ORIGINALS

NEW WRITING FROM
BRITAIN'S OLDEST PUBLISHER

Risk-taking writing for risk-taking readers.

JM Originals was launched in 2015 to champion distinctive, experimental, genre-defying fiction and non-fiction. From memoirs and short stories to literary and speculative fiction, it is a place where readers can find something, well, *original*.

JM Originals is unlike any other list out there with its editors having sole say in the books that get published on the list. The buck stops with them and that is what makes things so exciting. They can publish from the heart, on a hunch, or because they just really, really like the words they've read.

Many Originals authors have gone on to win or be shortlisted for a whole host of prizes including the Booker Prize, the Desmond Elliott Award and the Women's Prize for Fiction. Others have been selected for promotions such as Indie Book of the Month. Our hope for our wonderful authors is that JM Originals will be the first step in their publishing journey and that they will continue writing books for John Murray well into the future.

Every JM Original is published
This means every time you buy
not only investing in an author'
of (potentially!) valuable first e
we'd love for you to become part of our JM Originals community.
Get in contact and tell us what you love about our books. We're waiting to hear from you.

D1344955

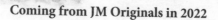

Coming from JM Originals in 2022

Catchlights | Niamh Prior
An unexpected novel that sets the innocence of childhood against
the violence of adulthood, the joys of passion against the horrors of
obsession and the reality of death against the magic of life.

Nobody Gets Out Alive | Leigh Newman
An exhilarating virtuosic story collection about women navigating
the wilds of male-dominated Alaskan society.

Free to Go | Esa Aldegheri
One woman's around-the-world adventure, and an exploration of
borders, freedoms and womanhood.

Catchlights

Niamh Prior

JM ORIGINALS

First published in Great Britain in 2022 by JM Originals
An Imprint of John Murray (Publishers)
An Hachette UK company

1

Copyright © Niamh Prior 2022

The right of Niamh Prior to be identified as the Author of the Work has been asserted
by her in accordance with the Copyright, Designs and Patents Act 1988.

A CIP catalogue record for this title is available from the British Library

Trade Paperback ISBN 9781529383430
eBook ISBN 9781529383416

Typeset in Minion Pro by Manipal Technologies Limited

Printed and bound in Great Britain by Clays Ltd, Elcograf S.p.A.

John Murray policy is to use papers that are natural, renewable and recyclable
products and made from wood grown in sustainable forests. The logging and
manufacturing processes are expected to conform to the environmental
regulations of the country of origin.

John Murray (Publishers)
Carmelite House
50 Victoria Embankment
London EC4Y 0DZ

www.johnmurraypress.co.uk

For my mother, who taught me how to read

Forecast

Have you ever been caught out in a surprise rain shower without an umbrella? Surely you have taken off your coat while playing in the sunshine on a warm day in winter, or wished you had one to wear on a chilly day in summer. Then you know that the weather here in the British Isles is unpredictable. Even the Meteorological Office can only forecast around twenty-four hours ahead.

Miss Havers does not allow me into her tearoom, but she lets me go around to the open back door like a stray cat. She has put a stool at the counter in the scullery for me. When she comes in, I hand her 7d in ha'pennies for tea and my empty flask. She nods and returns with a bowl of soup and a plate stacked with bread. The soup, thick with vegetables, has a swirl of cream at its centre, topped with a sprig of parsley.

'It would only go to waste otherwise,' she lies. I do my best to be ladylike though I'm possessed by the smell of the soup. She turns her back to me, leans against the jamb of the open door, looking out. I wolf into the food. After a while, when my chewing and gulping has slowed, she says: 'It's a fine sunny day today, isn't it? Do you think it will hold?'

I turn and look out and up at the sky. Mackerel tail high up. Stratus closing in from the distant west. 'Bring in your washing, Miss Havers.'

She checks on her customers, then goes outside to the clothes line and fills her basket with nearly dry laundry. She returns to the tearoom. I'm finished eating and the sky is a solid grey mass, so close it could touch our shoulders. She hands me my flask, now heavy with tea, and a wedge wrapped in tin foil.

'Black Forest gateau,' she says. 'For later. For saving my laundry. You've never been wrong yet.' It begins to spit rain. 'Stay here until it passes.'·She pats her curls and disappears again. I hear her talking with the ladies in the tearoom in hushed voices – too young to be living rough, outdoors does age the face, could be pretty with a scrub-up, if only . . . nice husband . . . take care of her – then the door shuts.

I close my eyes and listen to drops hit the windowpanes and the ground outside and the leaves that have recently begun to appear on the trees. There is no lullaby as soothing as the patter of raindrops. It reminds me of home, of falling asleep to the sound of rain on the windowpanes of the cottage and the flagstones outside. The wind coming in off the Atlantic. And I am back home in Kerry. I rise into the day and walk barefoot out along the cliff, lie down on a thick patch of seagrass, sink onto it like a springy new straw mattress. Sea pinks like fluffy lollipops nod beside me on their rigid stems. Ripples lap against rock and into small caverns, pushing the air out with wet slaps and gurgles. The sun is up and warming

2

the grass and if I could evaporate I would return as a soft drizzle that dampens the cheeks of children, I would land on tree leaves and seawalls and on stone roads, I would moisten worms brought to the surface by my falling, I would decorate flower petals and leaves with magnifying droplets, reflecting little worlds. Miss Havers coughs. 'You'll probably be wanting to move along now that it's stopped,' she says.

I catch a glimpse of myself in the window of Hartfield Haberdashery, but she is not me, that bag lady. No. Bag ladies are old and I am not old. I am young, but I carry my life in my bags. I go back to the river, the trees, as soon as I can, as soon as I have scavenged as much as I need.

My older brothers, boarding a boat to a dream life in America. We'll tell Elvis you were asking for him, they say. My grandmother Mamó outside our cottage, bent double like a tree leaning away from the wind into the peninsula, picking stones from the earth, hoeing, harrowing, always busy doing something, spreading seaweed, baskets of thick heavy brown bladderwrack and dúlamán, pungent with brine and displacement, sea louse and sandhoppers scurrying and leaping from it over the soil – thick impermeable foreign terrain.

Me, this body, sixteen years old, in a maid's uniform, in a big house in London. Yes, ma'am. No, ma'am. Meekly. Attic window my view of the world. From it I see a cockerel showing me from which way the wind is blowing – NW. Me in a maid's uniform, climbing out on the roof to taste the sleet, to feel the wind on my skin, to smell the freshness brought by it that chases away the stale, stagnant city air. One does not climb on roofs. Yes ma'am, sorry ma'am. One does not walk in the snow barefoot. Yes ma'am, sorry ma'am. A maid does not stand under the cherry blossom like a halfwit when there is company. Yes ma'am, sorry ma'am (oh but it is so beautiful, petals drifting like snow with every breath of breeze, catching on my uniform, gathering on the ground forming pink and white velvet puddles). One does not bathe in the fountain (oh but it was so hot and the water so cool). One does not work here any more.

I bathe in the river before the rest of the world rises. I bob with my eyes half-under half-over water. Some days the horizon is as straight as a ruler, as if man-made, but now sky and water bleed into each other, like blue ink on wet blotting paper. In school, blotting ink when I was supposed to be writing. Seeing pictures in their shapes. A storm once tore away part of the village on the cliff, before I was born. It took the church with it to the ocean floor. Me swimming at the beach near the smugglers' cave, with head under water so I can hear the church bells ringing.

In winter, nine winters now since the big house, I go to London where kind people take me into buildings with saints' names, give me a bed for the night when I feel the approach of rain, ice, snow. They give me food. Hot water to wash.

Sometimes I sit with my hat out in front of me where people hurry to and fro. Bus stations. Train stations. In the big city I incite sympathy, apathy, disgust in people and am ignored, pitied, humiliated, hunted down by volunteers with soup and blankets at times, but these emotions, these reactions I incite, they are theirs, not mine. None of it touches me. Invisible rings surround me, keeping me separate to them. They do not even look up except when the sky darkens or it rains.

Me in Hartfield in the spring. Abandoned boathouse my shelter. I come here by train with coppers I collected in the city. I didn't know where I was going the first time I came here. I boarded a train pointing away from the noise, the crowds, the big buildings, the imminence of stifling summer concrete heat. Down the line, I changed from that train to a smaller one. I got off where it was quiet, gentle, where land hugs the houses. There are ducks here – mallards and brown ones. They quack and waddle and get too close. My mother once said I was an ugly duckling, but I never grew into a swan. Just into me. She gave me to my grandmother when I was a baby. This village is a good place, full of good people. Along my walk, clutching my bags and my Black Forest gateau, the flowers are beginning to close up for the night. Pink-tipped daisies fold like upside-down umbrellas, close their yellow eyes.

A bearded fisherman near the boathouse that is my shelter. My stomach says no no no, go. But he tells me be a darling and pass him his net because he's holding a fish on the line. I turn, reach for it. Weight on my back, flips me over like a fish. Pins me down. Lying in the grass near the riverbank, I keep my eyes on the clouds and imagine as I used to when I was a child that it is me who is floating away, not the clouds. Those buttocks pressed into the mud are not mine, this place he jabs at is not mine. I am not this whispered word, 'bag lady'. The ducks have scattered. The clouds, greyish puffs of cumulus mostly, shape-shift from mouse into eagle.

Higher up, wispy mares' tails promise a change. And I would willingly transform now. Let me melt into dew on the grass, let the sun warm me with its rays, stretch them out like maternal tendrils and stroke me, heat me up, raise me up, turn me to vapour, be part of the air, let me ascend into the sky, cool, become a cloud, let my mass be weightless and expansive, undefined, divisible by breezes, let winds usher me along, calm, let me hover like a bird and white and grey as its feathers, take these teeth, this hair, these bones, make them all vapour, make them nothing but a haze, a mist and let it lift, let it rise all the way up there, up until there is no more up; return to the sea, fall into it or flow that way, down the estuary, become salinated, cleansed with salt, let all of this dirt, this grime that lodges in the skin wash away. The grease from my hair, memories from my body.

Afterwards, I wipe away the tepid wetness with dock leaves, pull my clothes back on. Gather my things back into my bags. Except the hospital bracelet. He gives me a sandwich. Later, I feed it to the ducks. Me, leaving the village. Heading for London. To the houses with saints' names.

Me, this body, twenty years old, in a hospital where it is warm, too warm and too dry and airless. It is too noisy with whines, screams, moans. My only comfort here is the sound of raindrops on the panes of glass like a lullaby, but this is torture too, because the windows don't open and have bars on them.

If I could open them a crack, I could let in some air, touch the rain and soak it up, become cloud and float away into the peace of the sky.

One kind doctor takes me from the ward in a wheelchair though I can walk. He gives me clothes to put on instead of the hospital gown. He wheels me outside to a garden and we sit together on a bench. He smiles when I slide my feet out of my shoes and nestle them in the grass. He nods to a gate, puts a purse of money in my lap, and leaves me there.

6

Summer in the city is too hot, but I am never alone with a fisherman here. All around are people busy going from train to train. Here underground there is no sunshine and the only breeze is that of the trains swooshing by. I sit and wait for the clinks in my upturned hat in this wormhole where day has been walled out.

Me in the Thames, next to the giant garden, upriver from the bustling streets. Float on my back, let the water turn me like a compass needle, like the compass needle in my gut. I always know which way is west; some things don't ever change. Like trade winds and cardinal points. I close my eyes and I am back in Kerry again. I climb down the cliff to where no one goes, no one knows, to the beach; in the cave I undress. Mid-tide. My feet meld into gravelly sand and shell, the shells yellow and every shade of brown and the dark purple ones, iridescent like jewels where outer layers have chipped off. Warm fragments of them stick in my skin when I lie on them and float off as I wade into the cold water. I feel a part of it, less apart than ever when my body meets the seawater, skin could dissolve and I and all my blood and organs turn the water red, my bones become sponge, red dissipating further and further, blanching with it as it does my name; the idea of me becomes no more than the echo of an oystercatcher's cry rebounding off ancient rocks, a high-pitched *pipeep* that diminishes into the soundscape, into the rhythmic shushing of waves over shoreline, of wind combing everything it touches, releasing the land's quiet voice.

Me in Kew Gardens, wandering flower to flower, barefoot, grass soft as the carpet in the big house where I was a maid, bags stashed under a bush. Freshly washed, clothes too. A summer dress too big for me, floating on the wind like a seed. One does not . . . but I do lie down. A black and red polka dot

7

bead making its way diligently from one blade of grass to the next. Why do you not use your wings? Where are you going on your tiny, busy legs? If it were black it would be a repulsive beetle, but a pretty coat makes all the difference in this world. The bug parts its shoulders, splits its back in half, two semicircles open like a bridge and black fly-like wings emerge, crisp and functional and fast and it's gone.

A man with a moustache talking to me. A kind man. It's safe, my stomach says. Scarlet pimpernel, the man says and points to the open blooms. Charles, he says, points to himself.

The breeze nudges me in his direction. I step closer and look at the flowers. Their petals twitch.

Look. I point west into the clear sky. Thunderstorm, I say, coming this way. We wait and watch until a dark anvil-shaped cloud climbing high in the otherwise blue sky appears. So there is, he says. Tourists surprised by the sudden tint to the light, the down-rattle of hail, the flashes and thunder.

It's okay, I work here, he says, leading the way. Gigantic palace made of glass, nothing but windows. Warm inside, but not like the hospital. There it was too warm and dry. Here it is pleasant. We watch the storm from inside, surrounded by palm trees and plants I've never seen before. Every lightning strike charges this body, these eyes open wide, breathe deeply, scrunch shoulders, arms, legs, in exhilaration. I turn to him and we count slow seconds until the thunder trembles up through our feet, wraps around us from inside and we quiver like dewdrops.

Security guard arrives, calling Charles aside. Whispering. I am not those whispered words.

She is not a bag lady. She is my new assistant. And her name is – he looks at me. My hospital bracelet. The one I left by the

8

river in Hartfield. The one that says 'Jane Smith'. That is not my name anyway. My name is – and I remember it and I am this body – it's Bláithín. My name is Bláithín. Bláithín is me.

In the calm, fresh smell of earth released by rain, everything is new and shining. Dust is washed away from leaves, now springing up as they shed drops, moving limbs. We sit in the sun together, soak up beams. Tell me about the cloud, he says. How do you know? I just do, I tell him. I feel it. You are like the scarlet pimpernel, he says. I stand up, close my eyes, spin around and around until dizzy. Stop, eyes closed I point. West. Wind at my back I lift my left hand, low pressure that way, I say. Tell me about tomorrow and if you're right, I'll give you a job. I look around, all around, and I close my eyes and I tell him.

He leads me to a white box on stilts that looks like a bee-hive. He opens one side of its louvred panels. Inside it has lots of gadgets, liquids that rise and fall inside tubes with the temperature, a cylinder that collects rain, dials with point-ers, mechanical arms that draw mountain ranges across rolling drums of squared paper, like the green line on the black screen in the hospital. This monitors the weather, he says. Is this a picture of its heartbeat? I ask. He smiles. You are not – he speaks the words aloud – a bag lady. You are a born meteorologist. It is beautiful, all of it, he says, isn't it, Bláithín? I run my fingers over the rainfall chart. I will make sure you see its full magnificence. Other climates, five continents. Places where the sun shines day after day after day and plants still thrive, thick and fleshy. Places where it rains all the time and the rain is warm and jungles sprout under it. Places where ice and snow never thaw and all the animals are white.

9

From one summer to the next he teaches me words that before I had only pictures for in my mind and feelings for in my body. He gives me a room to live in, a flat near the gardens. He teaches me to use the instruments. He pays me paper money for my work.

Autumn yielding to winter. Me on an aeroplane, in a new red coat with black piping. Charles's hand holding mine. The rumble of the engine and then the roar and leaning back in my seat, the ascent, and out the little porthole beside me the world turns into a train set with toy-sized everything and I rise up and up and up and all at once we are straight again and outside the porthole turns white, dotted with drops and all around the plane is white. I look at Charles. Yes, he whispers, yes. I put my finger to the window. Right there, an inch from my fingertip, is cloud. All around us is cloud.

Snow is the only thing here, where we landed in the Arctic. If there is anything else, it is deeply buried. All around us glows. I am tightly cocooned in a big fur-lined coat over my new red one, mittens and hat with goggles to protect my eyes. We travel on a snowmobile over hills and along a flat plain. In the distance is a dark patch and a stream of smoke rising. Drawing closer I see the dark patch is rounded like the roof of a shed. The snow has melted from it. There is a metal structure with aerials and a ladder up it beside the building. In front of it people are taking measurements with weather instruments. As we approach, they gather to greet us. We remove our goggles and shake mitten-covered hands like teddy bears meeting. Welcome, they say. You're just in time to help send off the weather balloon, one says to me. First a cup of tea.

Me, with my own telephone at a desk in London. At 9 a.m. it rings with calls and voices from stations all around the world. Telegrams and radios bring reports, too. Charles shows me how to map a picture of the weather with what they tell us. The world becomes a blue and green ball, swirled from above with a marbling of white, clockwise, anticlockwise, with black rings and arrows, red semicircles, blue spikes and numbers. Our pictures predict the future.

Another aeroplane brings me to the Amazon jungle where trees have shining leaves as big as people and all the wooden buildings stand on stilts. Take my muddy rubber boots off before climbing the steps and entering. Everyone bowing, smiling, smiling with their eyes, offering great slabs of red and yellow fruits. Men in towers keep watch with rifles. Cats big enough to eat us live here. Mosquitoes raise great welts on my skin and I scratch. In the mornings steam hovers up from all the mountains in view.

In Arizona, the heat is different. The sunshine is powerful. A special warmth that goes deeper than skin. A lifetime of dampness evaporates from me. No sea breeze. A complementary opposite that lived inside me all along. The flip side, the antidote to muddy parks and towpaths, to sleeping in sodden clothes and battling the night's cold, curled in a ball just to survive until sunrise. It's not like the heat of the hospital because this heat is everywhere. It's not kept in by windows and doors. It's expansive and it's in every brown and red thing I see, in every arid grain of sand. Me, warm, twenty-six years old. You like it here, says Charles. Yes, I reply. I am proud of you, he says. He returns to London. I stay.

In the evening, three new moons into my life in Arizona, I sit on my porch and watch the blood-red sunset hung with fluffy clouds from what little moisture the rays have burned up during the day. Just before 1 a.m. Chochokpi comes to help me check my Stevenson screen. His face is very serious as he follows all the instructions I have given him to read the instruments. We call in the results to Charles in London, where it is nine in the morning. When we have done this, Chochokpi stays a while, sits on the porch with me, looking out at the stars as has become a habit of ours. He no longer shyly runs away and I am at ease in his company. He tells me about his ancestors and he asks me about mine. When he goes I think about him until I see him again.

His serious look is gone the next day when in the waning heat of the late afternoon he tries to teach me to ride a horse. He laughs as heartily as the Hopi children, who gather around me while I sit nervously on the barely moving animal. I'm sorry, says Chochokpi through his laughter, as he leads the animal, It is our slowest, laziest horse! Then his face quietens and he points to a dark cloud. He puts his hand on my hip and turns me and the piebald horse to face east, our backs to the sun. He leaves his arm around my waist and leans gently against me as the cloud opens and a bright rainbow arcs over everything in my line of sight.

Captain Stamp

Stamp collecting is a hobby that is enjoyed by all ages. In fact, once you begin collecting you might never stop. There is much to learn about old stamps, and new designs are always being issued. You can pursue this interest on your own or join your local philately club to meet other enthusiasts.

The first part of Tegan that James fell in love with was her wrist. It was the only part of her he dared look at for at least five minutes that first morning in the sorting room. It looked so tiny and fragile and yet so efficient as it flicked letters into pigeonholes at almost the same speed as he worked. She was in the middle of a bundle when he arrived and not wanting to interrupt her, he'd sat down at his station beside her without saying a word. Second class blue, Basildon Bond. First class red, thick cream envelope as textured as a fingerprint. But her sweet perfume was as intoxicating as the sight of her dainty hands. His instinct was to pass out or run away, but he had to be someone he had never been before; he had to be the lad who reached out his hand when there was a gap in her work and said, 'Hello, I'm James.'

As she turned towards him, dark-blonde hair kicked away from her face in big bouncing curls, revealing a smile so eager it seemed it might burst her face. She took his outstretched hand and shook it tightly. 'I'm Tegan. I've just moved here from Wales.' Her stomach growled and she giggled, freckles dancing across her nose underneath her bright green eyes. James laughed, too. The others along the row – the old fuddy-duddies as James now suddenly saw them – were darting looks at him and Tegan, so they both turned back to work. First class red, second class blue, second class blue.

'There's quite a nice tearoom next door if you'd care to join me on your break. If you're hungry that is,' James said to the sorting wall.

'That would be lovely,' replied Tegan.

Rose's Tearoom was full of ladies with bags of groceries and parcels at their feet, in from their morning chores, whispering over scones with clotted cream and pots of Earl Grey. Tegan and James sat by a window, a lace curtain across its lower half concealing them from the street. He slipped a pipe out of the pocket of his new wool blazer and placed it on the table. He had absolutely no intention of smoking it, as the one time he had it had induced a spluttering coughing fit, but it looked good. He adjusted his new thick-framed tortoiseshell glasses and ran a careful palm over the wave of Brylcreemed hair above his forehead. He was settling into his new exterior.

'My full name is James Deane,' he said to her. For the first time ever that sentence brought not a stifled laugh but a look of intrigue. 'With an E at the end,' he continued. This was his chance, finally. A girl who did not know him. A girl who had

14

no context might actually consider him in her league and not below it.

'There is indeed a touch of James Dean about you. Are you a rebel, James?'

'Well, you'll just have to wait and find out,' he said, side-leaping the truth that he was the antithesis of a rebel, still living with his parents and in much the same manner as he did as a child. Turning attention away from himself he said, 'So tell me what brought you to Braintree?'

'I wanted a change from Monmouth, so I asked if the post office could transfer me to somewhere closer to London, and here I am. I was so glad to move! It's wonderful to be living away from my parents. Do you live with your parents, James? I'm living in a boarding house on the green, run by an old lady called Miss Clarke. She put me in the only ground-floor bedroom she has. Said she couldn't trust a man on the ground floor with a window for access – the Lord knows what time he'd be sneaking in and out, she said to me.'

Tegan continued to talk almost incessantly, taking short breaks to nibble morsels of scone. It took the pressure off James and he enjoyed listening to her, learning about her life in Wales, answering the odd question she allowed him time to answer. It was easy to play it cool by sitting, giving her his new, well-rehearsed lopsided grin. He prayed no one who knew him would come in and blow his cover. He had only just reached this stage of transformation; he'd grown out the dark hair he'd always worn cap-like, tight to his skull and traded in the thin metal-framed spectacles for tortoiseshell. He'd even managed to buy clothes for himself without hurting his mother's feelings. When he'd first learned the word *misperf*, when he was younger and getting into stamp collecting, he felt like he'd

15

found a word to describe himself. Now he felt things were finally beginning to change. He could make himself fit in.

'Would you like to go for a cycle with me this evening?' The words were out of his mouth before he had time to think about them. 'I mean to show you around, you know. There's a towpath by the river that makes for a nice cycle.' Oh God.

'Yes, I'd love that.' Tegan bounced in her seat.

He dared now to look directly at her, hold her flickering fern-green eyes, perfect inky circles.

As they cycled side by side, she laughed at his jokes and he was surprised to find he was being himself. This new exterior he'd built was becoming a part of him, no longer a disguise – he was growing into it. Of course he was entitled to the company of a pretty girl as much as anyone was. He'd left the schooldays far behind – over ten years behind. He'd had enough of making himself invisible. It hadn't been so bad in primary school. In fact it was good. He had friends then, in the philately club. During lunch breaks they would sometimes swap stamps. On Thursdays they had their official meetings and on those days he brought in an extra bag to carry his albums and catalogue.

He had started with just one general album, divided by countries, but his collection had grown so much that he had re-categorised them by theme. He had animals, transport, literature, sport. He could barely concentrate on his lessons on Thursdays, waiting for the meeting. Back then the boys in his class used to go over to his house to play and he was invited to birthday parties. But in secondary school all the boys he'd been friends with, even Nigel, who'd been a friend since before they'd started school, lost interest in stamps; they only had time for girls or cars or cricket. Then his father was the only one who shared his hobby.

It was their third evening in a row going for a bicycle ride, and this time Tegan had brought a blanket, a flask and a cake she'd baked. 'It's to thank you for being so kind to the new girl in town,' she said to James as she put the picnic in the basket of her bike. They stopped at a quiet spot a good way down the path, beyond where walkers normally went, and she spread out the blanket. He picked a white flower and handed it to her.

'Stitchwort,' he said. 'If you get a stitch, it'll cure it.'

'Really?' She lay back holding the flower up. 'Do I rub it on the stitch or eat it?'

'Oh, I don't know. I only know what it is because I saw it on a stamp once.' It was first in the third row down on the second page of his flora collection. A 1956 first-class British stamp.

'I think I should eat it,' she said and lifted it to her lips. 'Then again it might poison me. Oh well.' She spread her lips a little, smiling at him, feigning about to eat it.

'No, don't do it! You're too young to die!' He grabbed the flower and threw it aside.

'My hero. You saved me.' She put her arms up around his neck and drew him down. He kissed her. She kissed him. She took the glasses gently from his face and her eyes blurred like cancellation stamps on porous paper.

And so it continued, this dream in which he was winning. Spring was giving way to summer when he brought her to meet his parents. He was so proud of her. A yellow dress hugged her slight waist and flared down below her knees like the petals of a daffodil. She was so bright and vibrant in his parents' muted little home, like a shaft of sunlight streaming in through a crack.

When James was ten his mother sent him to Scouts, to toughen him up he later suspected, but he was lost when it came to all that outdoor stuff. The first time they had to camp out he'd spent a wakeful night terrified and cold and trying not to cry. He'd begged his mother not to make him go back and of course she didn't. 'He's a bit odd,' he overheard her say to one of her friends once, 'but we love him all the more for it.'

Tegan sat on the couch and looked around at the photos of him and his parents hanging on the walls. He thought she'd think it was all a bit twee and drab and old-fashioned, but she said she'd found the house charming, that it reminded her of her grandparents' house. He explained that his parents had adopted him when they were older, but she said it wasn't their age, it was something – she searched for words – 'something calm, something refined' in the house. 'Not like in my home,' she said as he walked her back to her place, 'with my teenage sister throwing tantrums and sulking and the place always buzzing with neighbours and relatives. It's enough to drive you mad.'

Sorting through a pile of letters at work he came to one addressed simply, 'To James Deane with an E'. On the back was a lipstick kiss across the seal. He looked across at Tegan. She was smiling mischievously while carrying on with her work. And so began a game of theirs of concealing love letters every now and then in each other's workload. He kept every one she wrote to him. He had always enjoyed his work from the moment he started: the stamps, the smell of paper, the sense of purpose, of being part of something as brilliant as the postal system, bringing messages from all over the world from one human to another. But now he loved it like never before.

It is difficult to imagine life without a postal system. But that is how it was until the General Letter Office was set up in the 1600s. Back then letters were relayed by Post Boys who walked or went on horseback and the person to whom the letter was addressed had to pay a delivery charge. The first adhesive stamps, the first in the world in fact, went on sale in England, in 1840.

Though James was thirteen years older than Tegan he didn't seem it; the two of them were known as the youngsters, and soon enough as the lovebirds, in the office. Every day they had cups of tea together and did crosswords on their breaks and in the evenings they cycled or went to the pictures and one night, giddy after going for a drink, Tegan pulled James in through her bedroom window and he finally learned everything he'd been missing out on.

He was on a high all the next day and could barely keep himself from smiling over at her at work and losing track of the letters he was sorting. After work they lay on their backs, side by side, on her blanket by the riverside.

'That was really something last night,' he said to her. He rolled onto his side and propped himself on one elbow to look her in the eyes. 'It was better than I imagined it would be.'

'It wasn't your first time, was it?' asked Tegan, sitting up slightly.

'Well...' James blushed as the realisation hit him that it had not been the first time for her. He felt embarrassed and also robbed of something, robbed of the experience he thought he had shared with the girl he loved.

'Oh don't worry, I only did it with one person before you. He was my boyfriend before I came here.'

James felt like he'd been kicked in the stomach. He looked down at the blanket and started picking at it.

'But he wasn't very nice to me. It turned out I wasn't his only girlfriend. I probably should have known that when he asked me to keep us a secret. But I thought it was because of the age difference. Oh, but you don't want to hear all about him, do you?'

No, James really didn't. And yet a part of him did. He looked up at Tegan.

'It's okay. Go on,' he said.

'Well, I think I only fell for him because he had a motorbike and – oh, that sounds shallow, doesn't it? No, I mean I thought he was a good man, too, you know, but . . . anyway, I left him behind with my old life. I like this new life much better.' She put a hand under his chin to raise his face, gave him a reassuring look and kissed him.

A week or so later when he'd been talking about how much he loved his work, she confessed that for her it was just a job. Just a means to an end, she said. A means to get away from home and live a little. Really what she wanted was to get married and have children and in her free time pursue creative hobbies. She admired how he made time for his stamp collecting and wished to find something she could apply herself to with such passion.

He wasted little time. Six months would be too soon he thought. She might smell desperation and bolt and he couldn't face being the old him again, being alone again, with just his parents for friends. He held out for a year. On the anniversary of her first day at work at the post office, he proposed to her in Rose's Tearoom and she said yes, yes, yes.

Once they married James and Tegan got a house in Cardigan Lane, a bungalow, gable end to the road, a window either side of the front door, looking out across the street at houses just like theirs. Tegan gave up work and turned into a fine cook and kept the house always in order, neat and tidy. James began to feel the sense of home he'd felt at his parents' house.

When a son was born to them, James felt his life was complete. He had everything he could wish for. They called the baby Ben.

Tegan worked hard bringing up Ben and keeping the house. Sometimes when James came home from work he got the impression that she was a bit tired and fed up. He suggested she attend a class, let his parents mind Ben now and then. After all, he'd said, hadn't she always said she wanted to do something creative? She took up knitting and knitted jumpers, waistcoats, hats and scarves, and when she'd run out of things to knit she took up sewing and then calligraphy and watercolours and finally photography. Ben spent more and more time at James's parents' house; they were doting grandparents and happy to help.

One day, while out for lunch with his beautiful wife, James bumped into Nigel. Nigel had turned from James's best friend in primary school into his worst tormentor in secondary school; that's the problem with letting people know you – they have all this knowledge they can use against you. As they approached Rose's Tearoom, Nigel was coming out of the door. James strode past, pretending not to see him. It would have been hard not to see Nigel as he was carrying a fishing rod and basket. Nigel approached him.

'James? James Deane?' Yes, he answered and introduced his wife, Tegan. Nigel seemed to have forgotten the hard time he used to give James, just talked and talked at him as if they were old friends. Back in town, he said. Got a business degree at university in London, and was taking over his father's shop and turning it into a supermarket.

Once you have your album, you can decide how to categorise your stamps. There are many ways to do this, for example by country or by theme. For example, a stamp depicting an illustration of a wolf in sheep's clothing could go into a section devoted to the country it came from but also into a section devoted to fairy tales or one devoted to animals.

Nigel then sort of latched on to James any time he bumped into him. Nigel recalled all the good times they'd had as children and James was warmed by this but remained cautious nonetheless. The teenage years were too fresh in his mind. Tegan invited Nigel around for dinner once. She said she felt sorry for him. She brought out the lace tablecloth and the wedding china. He arrived with two bottles of wine.

'Only the best for an old friend,' he said.

Tegan put James at the head of the table with her and Nigel either side, facing each other. Nigel drank three glasses of wine before the main course of beef Wellington and was soon divulging James's past.

'Captain Stamp, we used to call him, or Jimmy-no-mates . . . and remember your hair? Ha, Tegan, I swear he used to look just like that chap on the television . . . Spock, that's his name! Remember the time we went camping with the Scouts and you wet yourself inside in the sleeping bag? Ha ha ha!'

'No, I don't remember that,' James said. And he hadn't, until then.

Tegan put her hand on James's knee underneath the table and gave it a squeeze. He pushed it off.

'Still, he must've turned out all right in the end to bag such a lovely wife!' Nigel slapped James on the back and stared at Tegan, grinning, his teeth and lips black with wine, blending into his black beard that was reminiscent of Brutus from Popeye. He filled her glass with wine. 'You've done a fine job this evening, cooking us this delicious meal. I know how much hard work a woman puts into creating such a charming evening. You deserve to let go a little. Relax . . . unwind, enjoy some more of this fine vintage.'

And she did. She exhaled, kicked off her shoes and sank into her glass of wine, while Nigel explained to her, because of his hobby of fishing, how in tune with nature he was. When Nigel opened the second bottle of wine, Tegan jumped up.

'Music,' she announced. 'We need music.' She opened the record player and put on 'The Girl from Ipanema'. Nigel and James sat and watched while she danced and implored them to join her.

After that night, James and Tegan agreed to keep their distance from Nigel. Tegan suggested Nigel had only been wanting to wind James up in the way friends do, but James was adamant they would have as little to do with him as possible. They bumped into him from time to time, but never invited him round again. Tegan sometimes mentioned that she'd met Nigel in the supermarket and had a chat with him. After a while she stopped mentioning him at all.

Once you have your albums set up and you have some know-ledge of stamps, you will want to collect more. If you can easily get to the Strand in London, there are many dealers there, though most other towns have local dealers, too. If you keep an eye on the post you might even be lucky enough to find some interesting or valuable stamps on letters!

Six years into marriage Tegan was becoming increasingly restless and anxious. 'It's not you,' she'd say, 'it's this whole place. I don't know how to explain it.' Work was lonely for

James without her. Home became increasingly lonely for him, too. She was always out at her classes and clubs or meeting other housewives for Tupperware parties and the like. As Ben grew older he spent much of his time playing with other children out on the street. When Ben was in the house James tried to encourage him to take an interest in stamp collecting, but Ben got bored of it quickly and preferred to spend his time listening to Tegan's records with her.

James started to feel more at home at work than in his own house. Stamps were a comfort and a distraction, watching them go through his hands, all the blue and red ones with the queen's head in white, interspersed by foreign ones. Then one day, something came into his hands that caught his breath. It was a stamp with a picture of a steam train – he was familiar with it from the catalogue, but this one was printed in reverse. The letter it was on was addressed to Nigel at the supermarket. Nigel would never know the value of this stamp – it would just end up in the bin if James put it in the pigeonhole with all the others. The letter didn't look important. It was probably just some business correspondence that could be repeated or would never be noticed missing. Nigel owed him this much. James slipped the letter into the inside pocket of his blazer and continued sorting.

All human beings make mistakes sometimes, so when stamps are made they often have errors. These can take different forms, such as images being printed upside down or in reverse. Funnily enough, these mistakes can end up making stamps very valuable because of their uniqueness.

When Tegan was out that evening he filled a crystal bowl they'd got as a wedding present with warm water. He ripped the corner from the envelope and placed it in the water, watching it until the stamp began to peel away from the paper, its gum dissolving. It curled like an organism, like a bloom opening. He blotted it dry between sheets of paper, then laid it flat between two encyclopaedias to press it. A week later he took it out and began a new collection of found stamps.

To stick your stamp in your album, use a hinge. Fold the hinge and wet the gummed side so one half sticks to the stamp, wait a few seconds for it to dry, then stick the other half to the album. It is important to use good quality hinges so as not to damage the stamps.

That was the first. After that he collected more and more. He never found another erroneous one like that first one again, but he did collect some rare ones. Mostly though he collected ones he liked the look or colour or shape of. He had a section for trains, one for boats, and one for planes; one for literature, alphabets and languages; one for commemorative designs, flags, events; one for space exploration; one for naval vessels and one for insects.

The letters he held on to, with an aim to somehow get them to their addressees, but he never did. He just piled them up one after the other, stamp corners torn off, in a shoebox, then piled the shoeboxes up in the attic, where Tegan would never look. He kept the albums there, too. The more time she spent out of the house, the more he spent peacefully processing stamps and building up his collection or perusing his albums. He'd lean down, place the lens of his glasses to the glass of the magnifying loupe and lose himself in the tiny worlds of those designs, bordered by fringed perforations which he measured carefully with a gauge.

He tried to win back her affection, suggested going for bicycle rides and walks, but she looked at him differently. 'Why do you still wear that blazer?' she asked once as he was heading out to work. *Because it's the one I was wearing when I met you,* he wanted to say. *Because it made me more James Dean than Captain Stamp.* He shrugged.

He tried to encourage her in her hobbies. Photography seemed to be one that stuck. She was actually getting quite good at it, from what he could tell. She took some very good portraits of Ben and even some family portraits by using a timer-switch. He had his stamp albums and she had her photo albums – he hoped this meant that maybe they were growing together again. He bought her a lens for her camera for her thirtieth birthday. The latest one in the shop, a Nikon 50–300mm, F4.5. A brand-new model that year.

She broke down and cried. 'You are a wonderful, sweet man and I don't deserve you,' she'd said.

'Don't be silly,' he said, 'I'm the one who is lucky to have you.'

'No, really, James, I've treated you so badly.'

He shushed her with a kiss. They made love like they had in the early days and spent the morning together, lying in each other's arms as if newly in love.

Two weeks later she went out for a walk by herself to take photos. When she'd been gone an hour, James noticed her camera on the hall table. The chamber was empty and an unopened film roll sat beside it. She never came back.

In the past, special permission was given to cut stamps in half and use each half for half the value of the whole stamp. Such a half stamp is called a bisect.

Keepers

Once there lived a lighthouse keeper named Aron. His forefathers came from a land of ice. He was very handsome. His hair was the colour of sand and his eyes shone blue like a summer sea. Most of the time he lived in a striped tower that stood on a rock in the sea. He stayed in the tower for twenty-eight days at a time, always with two other keepers. The men could only leave the tower when a boat came to get them.

The rock with the tower was not far from land. On a clear day, Aron could see the cliff with the village from the lighthouse. On a day when the wind blew from the land towards the sea he could hear its church bells ringing.

One day, while he was on land leave for a week, he went for a walk on the beach below the cliff. There he saw a girl so beautiful that he instantly fell in love with her. Her hair was black as sealskin and her eyes were grey like a winter sea. When he talked to her she told him her name was Róisín. She was the daughter of a poor widow and she lived in a cottage near the village. She immediately fell in love with Aron.

They walked together on the beach. Róisín showed Aron her secret place. There were steps and a tunnel leading down into it from in the woods behind the cliff, but no one ever went there because it was quite far from the village. Aron was the first person she took there. By lamplight, he told her stories of shipwrecks and rescues. He explained to her that years ago this cave had been used by smugglers. He told her that once he heard of a shipwrecked crew surviving a violent storm because they sheltered deep inside such a cave, far back from where the sea could get to them.

At the end of his week off Aron returned to the lighthouse with the other two keepers. The most dangerous part of this journey was being lifted onto the rock, as they had to be swung up from the boat by a sort of crane. After a few days he got used to the daily rhythm of life in the tower. He and the other two keepers worked in four-hour shifts, while waves crashed at the base of the tower, and the wind wrapped around it. He polished the lens, wound the clockwork and kept watch over whatever sea craft came within view. He watched the horizon and skies and used observations for interpreting the weather the way his father had taught him. In fine weather the keepers painted the lighthouse and made repairs to it. They did all of the cleaning and cooking themselves. There was no mother or sister or wife there to do it for them. They kept the tower shipshape.

After a month, when Aron went on leave again, he was reunited with Róisín. Every day they went to her cave together. Then he went back to the lighthouse again for twenty-eight days and carried out his duties there.

The next time he was on leave he and Róisín sat down on the beach outside the cave. It was winter and so though it was only afternoon it was already dark. Róisín began to weep.

'I'm going to have a baby,' she said.

'That is wonderful!' said Aron.

'But I am young, and we are not married. My mother will surely kill me,' she sobbed.

'Do not worry, my little Rose,' said Aron. 'I will marry you before anyone knows you are with child.' He promised her he would find a job in a lighthouse on the mainland with a cottage at its base for them to make a home. 'We will raise our child and have more children and grow vegetables and keep chickens and a goat.'

Róisín smiled and wept, though now her tears were for joy. 'We will be so happy,' she said.

'Look, see how dark the sky is and how bright the stars,' said Aron. 'It is a new moon. We cannot see it now, but the moon will appear soon, and it will grow and become more beautiful every night until it is full and round and glowing, just like our baby inside you. I promise you I will be back on the next new moon and then we will be married.'

But it was winter then and the sea became wild and it took longer than expected for Aron to return. The waves were so vicious that no boat could get close enough to the lighthouse for the keepers to be taken off. Their food and fuel supplies ran low. At night Róisín walked the cliff and counted the seconds between the flashes of light coming from the sea. She pined for Aron and gently stroked her belly. It was two new moons before there came a calm, but it was a calm like no one had ever seen in winter. The sea was as still as glass. On land voices could be heard a mile away from where people spoke. Then came a snowfall and the village looked like a foreign land.

The boat arrived at the lighthouse. The relief keepers and plenty of supplies were swung onto the lighthouse rock. Aron and the other two keepers were transferred across still water onto the boat. Aron had an uneasy feeling and a strong urge to return to the lighthouse, but stronger than that was his need to see Róisín so he could marry her as soon as he could. So much time had passed already since he had seen her.

The wind came out of nowhere as they were making the journey from lighthouse to land. The sea was whipped by the wind and became an angry monster with a hundred hungry jaws. The boat was tossed around like a toy until it was swallowed by waves and dashed against the rocks at the base of the cliffs. Aron and the other two keepers were never seen again.

The wind blew on without mercy. It ripped the land apart. It wound down chimneys and blew embers from hearths, setting fire to the thatch of cottages. Stone walls crumbled and animals were swept away or frozen in the fields. The sea lashed at the cliff over and over until it collapsed into the swell.

Róisín was at home cowering with her two brothers and her mother, the widow. The wind howled like a wolf through the window and down the chimney. 'Take blankets and raincoats and follow me,' she said to her family. 'I know where we can go to shelter.' In the pitch darkness of the moonless night, the widow and the boys did not want to go outside. They said it was too dangerous. But when she told them about the cave, they followed. In the woods, branches cracked like kindling all around them and the wind bent the trees. They descended underground and there they remained all night. Underneath her shawls Róisín kept a protective hand on her belly and made a wish that her baby would know its father. She was afraid of her mother's wrath at finding out she was with child, and she was more afraid of losing Aron, so she wished that he was safe in his tower.

The lighthouse continued to flash its lights.

In the morning, when the wind had eased off, Róisín, her mother and brothers returned to the village. As they did, they saw that the entire church had fallen into the sea. Even the graveyard was gone. The edge of the land had receded overnight as far as the churchyard gate, a gate that now led to a sheer drop. Smashed boats lay on the land, and amongst the pieces of wreckage was part of the boat that brought the keepers home. Róisín wept with deep grief for she knew then that Aron was never coming back again. There would be no wedding and her child would have no father.

For months she stayed covered up in her cloaks and shawls, even when the weather grew warm. Unbeknownst to anyone living, underneath the layers her belly grew round and firm.

The baby came early. When the pains started, she went out to the cliff, into the woods, through the tunnel and down the steps into the smugglers' cave. Aron's spirit was there, waiting for Róisín. She gave birth to a baby girl. She washed her with seawater. When the baby opened her eyes, they shone like a summer sea. Aron's spirit surrounded the baby girl and went with her.

When Róisín's mother, the widow, saw her walking towards the village with a baby in her arms, she asked: 'Where did you get that?'

Róisín pointed to the beach.

'It must be a selkie baby,' her mother exclaimed. 'We must look for its skin so it can go home to the sea.'

Róisín and her mother searched the beach for a baby seal-skin but found none. 'Well, we cannot leave the baby,' said the widow, 'so we shall bring it home and raise it as a sister to you.'

And so, they took the baby home and named it Bláithín. Whenever Róisín was alone with Bláithín she fed her milk from her breasts. She wept at night when her mother took the baby away to sleep in a crib beside her. One day, Róisín's mother caught her giving her breast to the baby. She shouted at Róisín: 'You are too young to be a mother and you are not married. If you cannot be a sister to the baby then it will have to go and live with your Mamó, and she will raise it.' She grabbed the baby from Róisín. Then she locked Róisín in the bedroom. She left the cottage with the crying infant to take it to Róisín's grandmother. Aron's spirit went with Bláithín.

Róisín wept every day after she was separated from Bláithín. She did not eat, and she grew weak. She spent her days down on the beach near the cave and told her mother she was look-ing for Bláithín's sealskin so that they could return her to the water. She went into the sea every day because that was where Aron was. A few weeks after Bláithín had been taken away to live with Mamó, Róisín stayed too long in the cold sea. She caught a chill and died.

As baby Bláithín grew into a little girl, it wasn't at home in Mamó's cottage that she felt most at ease but outside on the cliffs, in the woods or down on the beach. She spent a lot of time lying in fields or on the strand, looking straight up at the clouds; she observed their shapes, their colours, their height and the speed at which the wind pushed them along. She'd imagine it was her who was moving, not the clouds, that she was the one flying to some other part of the world. She wondered what clouds felt like, what they tasted like, what it was like to be in the middle of them.

Something – a warmth in her gut, a knowing in her head, a belonging – drew her outdoors, led her to observe the winds, the signs of the changes about to come in the weather. She knew when it was going to rain. She could not read words very well – she did not pay attention at school – but she could read the clouds, every shape and shade, she could even read clear skies and breezes and she could close her eyes and imagine the whole thing – heat, clouds, wind, water – and she could tell what weather was coming the next day.

Late one summer's night when Bláithín was a little girl she went for a walk by the edge of the sea. It was a dark night, a new moon. She was not allowed out after dark but when Mamó slept she slept soundly. The bottom of the half-door had a loud squeak, but the top did not, so Bláithín used a stool to climb out.

She found her way by heart, knowing every rise and fall of the ground, every rock and mud-worn path, every gorse bush. The flashes of the lighthouse guided her. They were a constant, a comfort in her life.

She walked in the tideline letting her feet get used to the temperature of the water. Every now and then one of the ripples rolling in shone with a greenish light. When she lifted her foot, it left behind a print that glittered for a moment. Bright glowing specks where she had stood lit up and went out. She walked back and forth making glowing footprints. She balanced on one foot and splashed with the other in the water. Drops glowed as they hit the surface. She dropped her nightdress on the dry sand and waded into the water, sloshing and sprinkling it with her hands. She marvelled at specks of light sliding down her body and in that moment she knew she was taken care of, she knew there was magic, and even though she sometimes stood on thorns and bled and even if Mamó was sometimes cruel to her, something she could not name was with her to help her through it. She felt it in the instinct that had led her there. She felt it when she lay and looked up at the clouds.

Aron's spirit stayed with Bláithín and vowed to stay with her until it was certain that she would live happily ever after.

Life of the Honey Bee

Though the worker bees are female, they cannot lay eggs – only the queen does that. It is the workers' job to look after the queen, feed her, keep her and the hive neat and tidy and protect it from intruders. They gather nectar and pollen from lots of different types of flowers and take care of the eggs and larvae, too. Without them the colony could not survive.

She runs her fingertips over the blister pack, the hollows where collapsed foil and concave plastic meet. The resistance of a full cell – pushes gently until pop, one side bursts and the tablet slides into her waiting palm. She used to only take them for social occasions or for stressful days. She's not even leaving the house today. She hasn't left the house in weeks. She washes the tablet down with the end of the glass of white wine she had with lunch. If there is one thing she loves about au pairs, it's that they are refined enough not to judge her for having wine during the day. They come from sophisticated cultures – sophisticated enough to know the benefits of a glass of wine with lunch. Not like that local woman she had before. They are sometimes surprised to find themselves au pairs to older children, but someone has to drive the teenagers to hockey practice and their friends' houses and she needs help with cooking and cleaning, too. Three au pairs and each au pair has three children to look after. They don't even have to live in the house. They share the apartment above the garage. It's much easier to assign the au pairs equal amounts of children since her eldest, Fergus, moved out three years ago to go to college in Galway. Ten is such a tricky number of children to divide up, nine is much easier. Sometimes she mixes up their names, but some of the young ones look like the older ones did when they were young so it's easily done. She finds it easier to remember them in threes: Orla, David, Carol, the teenagers; Malcolm, Brendan, Linda the middle ones; Patrick, Simon, Helen the small ones.

The morning time she usually spends in the main part of the house. It's only herself and the au pairs then, with Declan off at work and the kids all at school. She loves this time of day and so do the au pairs. She treats them like grown-ups, acts as if they are friends of hers who've called around for a chat. They all sit around the kitchen table and she talks to them about their boyfriends and tells them all how pretty they are. They make milky coffees and hot chocolates and bake pastries and she compliments them on their skills in the kitchen. After their morning get-together the au pairs make sure the place is spotless before they go to their various duties.

The hive contains a remarkable cell, unlike any of the others, built especially for the queen bee. Its walls contain a lot of pollen and it is sealed over until she is ready to come out.

Anaïs will be home soon with the youngest ones. Then Veronique with some of the older ones and later Odette with the others coming from sports practice, piano lessons and one from college. She pours herself another glass of wine, disappearing it in two gulps. She hears a car in the driveway. Avoiding windows, she walks from the kitchen, through the utility room, down the corridor to her sitting room and clicks the door shut just as she hears the front door open. This room is off bounds to everyone. She exhales, kicks off her slippers and runs her toes through the soft-pile carpet.

She decided early on that she needed her own space, away from hands that smear chocolate and yogurt and jam on things, away from prying fingers and eyes, away from little voices asking incessant strings of whys and later, crackling teenage voices proclaiming the unfairness of everything. So, she'd had an extension built. The room holds a bookcase, a plush couch, a television and has a solid wooden door.

That door is magic. It erases the sound of school bags being thrown down, the moans and excitement at the end of the school day, the rattling of cutlery and crockery as they descend upon food cupboards. It shuts out the shouts and yelps and giggles. It blocks out the horrendous sounds of indie or grunge or whatever it is they're listening to now as they take over the tape player with their cassettes. It keeps out the grassy odours of the young ones and the Lynx and Impulse of the older ones.

She switches on the TV to the soap she pretends is her programme. It's just a more favourable form of noise than their chatter and is her excuse for being in there (*shh, your mum's watching her programme*). She pushes a few John Grishams aside on the bookshelf to get to the booze behind them, pours herself a honey liqueur and sits sipping it staring at the movement on the screen, the colours, without keeping track of the story. Her own thoughts are all she hears.

She's nicely numb by the time Declan gets in from work. She puts on lipstick, slips into her high heels and walks to the front door to greet him, a gesture he doesn't realise she does out of mockery – her, the perfect housewife, ha! He hangs his coat and smiles to see her every time. Not a clue that she is laughing inside.

Sure, she used to be the perfect housewife – and for a while she even wanted to be. For those first few months after they were married when she was pregnant. She'd decided to try to be the person she'd fooled him into thinking she was. The naive sweet girl who wanted nothing more than to raise a family and make a good home. She took up sewing and crochet. She made blankets and booties. Once she got to nesting there was no stopping her. She redecorated the whole house. She even put up a picket fence and painted it white.

As head girl at boarding school she had her own room. It was constantly teeming with other girls who came to bask in her company and revel in her flattery. *June, you're so good at doing nails. I can never get it right. Oh Mary, you could be a hairdresser. No one else can iron my hair the way you do. Turn up the radio, Bernadette, this song is so good.* Then the other girls would all love the song too until she decided it was no longer hip. She had opinions about everything and announced those opinions with such conviction that the others knew better than to question her.

One night as she held court to a circle of pyjama-clad girls in her room, she declared, 'I'm going to Glasgow after the exams – for the whole summer! You've all got to come with me. It'll be amazing! We'll have a blast! My dad knows someone who has a flat they're going to rent us cheaply. We'll all get jobs waitressing. My dad is giving me a Morris Marina for my eighteenth! I'm driving all the way to Glasgow! You have to come with me. It'll be the best summer of our lives!'

One of the girls asked dubiously, 'Glasgow?'

'Yes,' she said with enthusiasm. 'We'll go to all the best music venues. We might even bump into Gerry Rafferty! Oh, and we'll go on day trips to Edinburgh and see all the sights in Scotland!' She gave mini-claps with her hands and bounced like a child with excitement. 'Think of all the handsome men with their sexy Scottish accents!'

The girls all laughed and privately entertained the notion that they would go too, that it was possible to get away from their families for a summer, that it was a good idea. She decided they should celebrate with a midnight feast.

'Mary, sneak down to the kitchen and steal some biscuits for us, will you? Oh, go on, you're so petite and graceful. I could never be as quiet as you.'

A week later, she sat on her bed and announced, 'Girls, there's not quite as much space in my car as I thought. I have to bring Brian Deasy with me as well. I couldn't get out of it. Some of you might have to get the bus and go as foot passengers on the ferry, but we'll definitely all still go. And some of you might have to find another place to stay, too, because Brian's taking a room in the flat.'

'But I spent all week convincing my parents to let me go, and they're only letting me go on condition there's somewhere for us all to live,' said June.

'I told my boss at the restaurant that I'm going to be away and now he's given my job to someone else,' said Mary.

'I turned down a job minding our neighbours' children,' said Bernadette.

'Don't worry, we'll figure it all out, girls,' she assured them.

One by one over the next few weeks she filled the girls' places in the car and in the flat with boys instead of them.

The virgin queen bee must find a husband. To do this she goes on her maiden flight when she is young. There are plenty of males in the hive, but she won't mate with them there. She goes away instead, flying high up in the air, and the males from her own hive and neighbouring ones follow her. She is so strong and fit that only the healthiest, most robust drones manage to stay in pursuit of her.

'I feel I've always connected more with fellas, you know?' she said as she invited Shane, captain of the neighbouring boys' school rugby team. They stood in a queue at the shop that was between the grounds of both schools.

Shane nodded, staring at her lips.

'You know, I think men get me more than girls do. They're more straightforward, you know?'

The queue jostled as a few lads poured in and she was pushed up against Shane.

'Yeah, definitely.'

The day before she left for Glasgow she went to the hairdressers. 'I want a new look. Something less . . . Irish looking,' she requested.

The hairdresser held out a card with colours on it.

'That's it.' She smiled and pointed at a loop of synthetic hair stuck to the card. 'Honey.'

The hairdresser went into the back room for the chemicals and she smiled at herself in the mirror. Yes, honey-coloured hair was what she needed. And a fringe.

Next day she drove up to the school gates where she'd arranged to collect the lads. When she emerged, decked out in yellow flares and a black crochet top, she swished her hair around her with a flick of the head and the lads all wolf-whistled. She beamed and said: 'I have a new name. From now on, you will call me Honey.'

They guffawed but stopped immediately when she stared at them. 'I will only answer to the name Honey. Or no one gets in the car.'

'It's a pretty groovy name, really,' said Shane. 'Honey.'

'Yeah, I can dig that,' said Tony.

Brian nodded. 'Honey it is.'

They all threw their bags into the boot and got in. Tony and Brian in the back seat. Shane opened the driver's door for Honey. As she brushed past him to sit in, he whispered 'You look amazing.' She smiled and kissed him on the cheek. The other two were oblivious to this, busy trying to fit themselves between Honey's bags in the back seat.

On the road they sang along to the radio, smoked cigarettes and imagined what adventures lay before them. When no one else was looking Honey caught Tony's eye in the rear-view mirror and gave him a wink. She did the same to Brian. All three of the young men were in high spirits thinking they were the chosen one.

Two weeks after arriving, all four of them were out in the car near the river, swigging from bottles of whiskey in the early hours of the morning. They hung out of the windows shouting and laughing. Shane drove while Honey opened the passenger door and stood, holding on to the roof. He reversed, catching the door on a stone bollard.

'Oh, shit.' He was pale. 'I'm so sorry, Honey.'

She got out and looked at the car, its passenger door hanging from it like a broken wing, and burst into hysterical laughter.

'Come on, let's do the other one, so they match!' She made Shane sit in the passenger seat and she got behind the wheel herself. She got them to direct her into another bollard, nearly ripping the open driver's door from its hinges. Then she aimed the car at a slipway and drove halfway down it.

'Let's take the car for a paddle.' She giggled.

'Let me out,' said Tony, and Brian followed him out of the car onto the slipway. Shane got out, too. It was just Honey in the car.

'Chickens!' she shouted at them. She drove the front wheels into the water.

'Honey! Stop,' Tony called. She got out and looked around.

'Let's see if it can swim,' she said. She leaned in, released the handbrake and quickly withdrew. The car rolled into the river and they all stood watching as it bubbled and filled with water and slowly, then rapidly, sank.

Honey sat on the slipway doubled over with laughter. She took a swig from the bottle and waved goodbye to her car.

'Now that is outta sight!'

'How are we going to get home?' asked Shane.

'Lads, we've got to be up for work in three hours,' said Brian.

Honey hadn't bothered to find a job. She had intended on it, to be like the others, but the reality of it was too much hassle. So instead she told any new people she met that she was a waitress and had a day off. It was much easier to fit in by pretending you had a job than to actually get one. She was more interested in going out at night and meeting new people. Exciting people. The boys from home were turning out to be a bit of a drag. Plus, they'd all started bickering with each other.

As the males fly after the queen bee, one or more of them catch up with her and mate with her. People used to believe that the queen bee had only one mate, but studies now show that as many as ten or fifteen drones could mate with her.

She sat, topless, on the carpet in her room between Craig and Jimmy, the two shipbuilders she'd met in the bar. The room glowed orange from the streetlamp outside and the candles inside. The air was filled with the smell of incense and pot. She'd put on her Stealers Wheel record and dropped the needle at the start of 'Stuck in the Middle with You'. She leaned towards Craig, kissed him slowly while she held Jimmy's hand. Then she kissed Jimmy while Craig slid his hands around her waist. She put her hands down to meet his, stroked them, then unwrapped her tie-dyed skirt and smiled at them both.

The party was still going on in the sitting room but over the music she could hear loud noises through the wall from Tony's bedroom next door. Crashing and banging. The slamming of wardrobe doors. Soon she lost awareness of any sounds as she gave her body over to pleasure.

She didn't know when the record ended, just that there had been silence but for the slow whirr and crackle of the turntable when they were finally still, a tangle of limbs. She lay between them for a while until she was sure their breathing was that of sleep. Then she walked into Tony's room and found it bare. All the drawers were open and empty. His key was on the bedside table. She climbed into his bed and pulled the blanket up over her. She'd miss him. It was a pity he'd left so abruptly. Brian and Shane had gone back to Ireland weeks ago. Maybe Tony thought he was her boyfriend because he was the only one who had stayed on with her. But that didn't make her his girlfriend. Here in Glasgow, she felt freer than she had ever felt before. Here she was in a city and a country where no one knew her. She could do what she wanted without having to be the head girl, the good girl, without having her every move scrutinised, without having to be on her best behaviour as the daughter of the owner of the biggest department store in the city. Here away from watchful eyes, she could be anyone she wanted to be. She wasn't about to tie herself down by doing a line with a local boy from back home.

There is no mistaking the queen bee in appearance. She is more lustrous and sleek than the other bees and her legs are orange-brown. In her movements she is measured and regal.

'Thanks for coming, Princess,' her father said. 'You know I hate going to these things. It wasn't too bad when your mother was alive but going to them by myself is torture.'

A soft-looking man, with thinning dark hair, glasses and ruddy cheeks, shorter than her in her heels, the suit seemed a contradiction on him, too strict and angular for his body. Honey smiled down at him.

'Well, Daddy, it's not like you can get out of it. You are the boss.'

She entered the hotel function room in Dublin linking arms with her father. It was the end of September and she'd just returned from Glasgow. She surveyed the round tables full of employees dressed up in their finery, and the stage with the podium. She wore an olive-green tweed skirt with a matching twinset. A string of pearls sat on her collarbone and her hair was pinned up in a French roll.

Her father's speech was powerful. After dinner they made the awards. Highest sales, most new clients, best window display and then the novelty ones: worst timekeeper, best hairstyle and so on. Honey sat beside her father at the main table and clapped and smiled for all of them. At the end came the award everyone was eager to win some day: the employee of the year.

'You'd be amazed how everyone ups their performance in July and August,' her father had often joked at home. 'Like children behaving themselves before Christmas.'

'And the winner is . . .' Her father behind the podium pulled a card from an envelope. 'Declan Moran.'

Her father presented the plaque and the bonus cheque to the young man. Declan had been in her school, in the year ahead of her. He had always been quiet. Out of school uniform and in a suit, with long hair now, he was quite handsome. He'd grown into himself. In school he'd been awkward. Anytime she'd spoken to him, or rather at him, he'd blush. She'd known he'd fancied her and toyed with this knowledge, walking almost completely past him in the corridor, then turning at the last second and staring into his eyes saying 'Hello, Declan' without giving him time to respond, flipping her head forward again. Knowing he was watching her walk away she'd add some sway to her stride, sure she had sent his blood rushing not just to his face.

Now here he was, a year into his job with her father's company and winning the most coveted award already. She stood up and went up on the stage – as she had not done for any other prizewinners – shook his hand and kissed his cheek. He returned to his seat and she watched him as he walked, the fashionable suit with wider lapels than anyone in the room, bright-green shirt with matching paisley tie. He took out a pipe when he sat down, packed it with tobacco, lit it with a match and puffed.

While everyone mingled after the ceremony, she sidled up to him, smiling. He returned her look with as much confidence.

'All right so,' she said.

'All right so, what?'

'All right so, you can take me out. I'm free tomorrow night. You can collect me at seven.'

He tilted his head, looking at her with curiosity, grinning. He let her wait in silence just long enough for her smile to waver.

'I'll see you tomorrow at seven then.'

He kissed her hand, then turned to continue accepting congratulations from his colleagues.

After her wedding flight, the queen bee returns to the hive where she settles down and devotes the rest of her life to laying eggs.

On their third date he took her to a pub after the pictures. Some of the older men stared to see a woman in a bar but she took no notice. Soon a crowd of young people came in and then there were almost as many women as men in the place. Declan held her hand across the dark wooden table.

'You know I always liked you in school.'

'I had no idea,' she said. 'You were so quiet.'

46

'Well, school is a strange place. I feel like I wasn't really me until I left it. Out here in the world the playing field is level, do you get what I mean?'

'Mm.'

There was a silence between them for a while. Bob Dylan's 'The Times They Are a-Changin'' played on the radio. She remembered swaying and singing along to it just a few months before at a party in Glasgow when she had been freer than ever and felt more herself than ever.

'You know I'm going to inherit my father's business?' she said.

'Are you now?'

'Yes. I'm the only child. In fact, he's already begun transferring things into my name.'

'Well, good for you, but you know nobody likes a show-off. If you're trying to impress me . . .'

'I'm pregnant.'

He stared at her.

'But we . . .' he began.

Silence hung between them until Declan gave a slow nod and released a deep breath.

'I see,' he said.

They finished their drinks without another word, him puffing on his pipe and her looking at the group of young people around their own age, singing along to the Beatles' 'Ob-La-Di, Ob-La-Da'.

He did not lean over to kiss her when he dropped her home. He said in a neutral tone, 'I'll ring you tomorrow.'

The wedding was the opposite of the one she had always dreamed of. It was small. The fewer people at the wedding, the fewer there would be doing calculations when the baby was born. She could let relatives assume that they'd been sweethearts since school. She could even pass this story off to her father, and he would believe it because he wanted to.

Despite the low-key ceremony, she had her dream dress, which she designed herself and had made especially, and the chapel was an ancient one on an island in the middle of a lake. She was not about to let circumstances get completely in the way of her day. Even if those circumstances meant she had to have the dress let out twice because she was rapidly growing with a set of twins inside her.

The only job the queen has is to lay eggs to create more worker bees or queens. She leads the colony with quiet, peaceful grace, rarely leaving the protection and darkness of the hive. The workers take care of feeding and cleaning her so that she can focus all her energy on her vital task of laying eggs.

Six months later she held the squirming Fergus in her arms.

'I want to have another baby,' she said to Declan. He looked at her with concern.

'You've been through a very traumatic experience. I think we should wait a while. Take the time to grieve over Robert. And to get used to being a mother to Fergus.'

'No, I'm ready. You're the breadwinner. This is my job.'

She'd secretly hoped that somehow she could create a new version of baby Robert by having another child. Although his twin was alive, he was not like him at all.

'Ate all his brother's food,' is what the nurse said when Fergus had come out alive and fat and his brother a shrunken thing, light as an angel's feather, lifeless and still, while Fergus bawled, turning puce.

She'd tried not to hate Fergus. She tried to love him but every time she looked down at him she felt a sting. She learned that all those things that are meant to come naturally to mothers did not come to her. She felt cheated that no one told her you don't always love your children from the moment they are born. Not all of them.

And sometimes she felt maybe she'd brought it on herself. But she could not contemplate that for too long.

'Declan, I need to. I need to know that it's possible to love your children the way you are supposed to.'

'Don't say that, Honey, we've got a perfectly good son here, waiting for you to love him.'

'I try . . . I do try. It's just every time I look at him . . .'

'I know.' Declan held her.

She had another baby. And another. And another. If she couldn't be out in the world being beautiful then she would be the best at what she was. She would rule her own hive. She was good at having babies. She got no sickness at all. In fact, she felt more alive when she was pregnant. Purposeful. She loved how people told her she glowed. She loved having au pairs around to help her and revere her. She loved how strangers gave up their seats for her and let her move to the front of queues. A married woman didn't get much attention, but a pregnant one did. She had nine more babies after the twins.

Declan never asked about that summer and she never told him. She never told him about how she'd almost found herself. How for once in her life she'd felt like she didn't need to set trends by secretly following others, how for once she'd felt real. Maybe to an outsider she'd been promiscuous and out of control. She'd acted in a way she never could in her hometown, but inside she'd felt more like herself than she'd ever done before. She often talked to her au pairs about her one wild summer in Glasgow. *This is just between us, girls, of course,* she'd say.

In her sitting room, its closed door keeping the world out, she slides her hand down between the cushions at the back of the couch and pulls out a small silver photo frame. She sits, holding it with both hands, in a trance. From the baby's expression he could be sleeping. But there is something else to it, something at once pained and angelic. Eyelids that never opened to the world. Sweet, sweet boy, Robert, her first born. Over twenty years since his brief visit to this world. He looks like he's made of candle wax, an unpainted doll, too pale, tinged with blue. So many times since then she'd asked why. Even his healthy twin brother Fergus, born moments after him, was no consolation. She wondered sometimes if it was her free-spirited actions that brought such a fate on her first born, a sort of karma. Was it possible Robert had come from Jimmy and Fergus from Craig? Clutching the picture to her chest she sobs like it only happened yesterday, alcohol blurring the lines of time.

That picture of Robert was the only photograph she owned from the day of his birth forward. Every photograph after that was a stab to her heart, a finger twisting in the wound. The empty spaces where Robert should be taunted her every day. She banned photos. Not outright, no. But when family or friends gave them presents of photos she put them in drawers and gave away the frames. When Fergus left to study photography, she could stand him even less.

'Don't you ever worry that you'll favour one over the rest of them?' her hairdresser – who had only one child – asked one day as she was dyeing her hair for her in the kitchen.

'No, I hate them all equally!' she'd responded. The hairdresser and the three au pairs all laughed.

It was a joke, of course, but she meant it a little bit too. She hated them all for not replacing Robert. And when each one was born and began to develop their own little personality, she passed them more and more into the care of au pairs. Two of the children spoke their first words in French and were now fluent and three of the older ones had a good grasp of the language, so she could say she was doing it for their education.

The hairdresser was not the only one who came to the house. She had beauticians who carried out all sorts of treatments and stylists who helped her to choose what to order from their catalogues. Sometimes her daughters would gather round her, as well as the au pairs, when these people were in the house and she'd let them stay as long as they were quiet. They'd sit in awe and were thrilled when they were allowed to try on some lipstick or nail varnish. But as soon as the service people were gone they had to wipe it all off again. She was the only female in the house allowed to wear make-up. The teenagers whinged about this. 'When you pay the bills, you can make the rules,' she'd say to them and once she heard Carol, or maybe it was Orla, whisper under her breath, 'She doesn't even pay the bills. Dad does.'

The day before the twins' twenty-first birthday, she locks herself away in her sitting room. She stays there all afternoon, sipping vodka and staring at the silver-framed photo of baby Robert. At midnight she begins to weep. She slides from the couch to the floor, turns on her knees to face the couch, as if about to pray. She lifts a flap of material and pulls out a suitcase. She opens it, shuffles the items inside around, taking a mental itinerary. Toiletry bag complete with doubles of all the cosmetics and make-up she has in the main bathroom, seven pairs of knickers, seven pairs of socks, three bras, a few simple items of clothes: slacks, blouses, cashmere jumpers and a skirt she'd worn that summer in Glasgow, a wrap one with swirling tie-dye pinks and purples and blues. She knew she'd never wear it again but picking it up and holding it reminded her of who she once was. It brought her back to herself and gave her the courage to keep packing items one at a time; it gave her the courage to dare to have this suitcase. She might never use it but having it was comfort enough that she could use it. The potential to leave lay there underneath her couch all the time.

Declan knocks at the door.

'You coming to bed?' His voice is muffled through the wood.

She closes the suitcase and slides it back under the couch.

'We've got a big day tomorrow. Fergus is coming in the morning and I want to set things up for his birthday party.'

She slides the photo frame down behind the cushion, stands, switches off the light, closes the door and follows Declan to the stairs. He ushers her ahead, walks behind her, keeping an eye on her bumbling gait as she climbs the steps with the effort of a mountaineer.

'Fergus doesn't even want a party,' she says.

Bees sting, to defend their colony or when they feel trapped. If you want to handle them you must know how to avoid vexing them.

In the bedroom, she sits and sobs. When he puts his hand on her shoulder, her head snaps up, a look of accusation on her face.

'Admit it! You were relieved he died, weren't you?'

'Oh my God, not this again. How can you even say that?'

'You never really wanted to bring them up. I bet you thought it was some sort of divine retribution.'

'Shh. You'll wake the whole house.'

'Don't you dare shush me. I'll give you shhh!'

She stands up and slaps him hard across the face. She wobbles and loses balance, landing with her hands on the dressing table to steady herself. He rubs his reddening cheek.

'You want to hit me, don't you?' she says smiling. 'But you can't hit a girl.' She slaps him hard across the other cheek and laughs.

He puts a hand to that cheek and takes a step backwards. 'Let's talk tomorrow, when you're sober.'

'No, let's talk now!' She flings both arms up in the air.

'Why don't you get some sleep?'

'I'm not tired.' She squares up to him, staring at him with bloodshot eyes.

Sighing, he sits down on the bed and gets under the covers, pretending to fall into an instant asleep. She staggers downstairs, puts on a Stealers Wheel tape and turns the volume up loud.

In the morning she stays in bed. Declan brings her up liver salts and a glass of water. When she comes down around lunchtime Fergus is in the kitchen with Declan, the teenagers and the au pairs. The younger kids are all outside, playing in the garden. Holding her temples, she looks at Fergus.

'Happy birthday,' she says to him in a low voice. When he stands up to hug her she puts her hand up as if to stop traffic.

'I think I might be coming down with something. Don't come too close.'

Studies in Plastics

When plastics were first invented, a lack of knowledge about how to produce them led to many faulty products. Nowadays, we understand that plastics are new materials with their own uses, and items made from them are carefully designed.

I'm scouting in the ward the day the vagrant woman arrives. I feign checking information on clipboards as I watch her from the other end of the room. She is quite docile until she sees the bars on the windows. Then she tries to turn around, but two orderlies have her by the arms and they haul her through to the corridor at the other end.

'Please let me go,' she implores in an Irish accent.

'Shh, love, c'mon, you're all right,' says a nurse, beckoning her from the corridor with an encouraging wave of the hand and a nod of the head. 'You'll feel much better after a hot bath.'

As they drag her past me I take a quick mental inventory. It's hard to tell what her body is like underneath all those clothes, but she appears neither under- nor overweight. No visible scars or deformities. Inoffensive facial features. She is of little use to me, and I of little use to her. A bed and hot meal are probably all she needs to iron out her mind.

The other patients take no notice of the commotion. They have their own struggles. Some lie in bed, some sit rocking, others mill around; some are silent, some moan like babies, others babble away in conversation with each other or themselves.

One woman has burn scars all down the right side of her face and neck. She's around my age, in her early thirties, I estimate. I sit on her bed. 'How are you today?' I ask. She turns away. I take a mirror from my pocket and hold it up in front of her. The second she sees herself in it she shouts in horror and cries, covering her face with her hands.

A nurse comes over to us and puts an arm around the woman. 'Did the doctor upset you?' she asks. I slide the mirror back into my pocket.

'I'm putting this patient down for surgery with me,' I announce. I look at the patient. 'How about that?' I ask her. 'How about we tidy up that face of yours? Then you can get your mind back in order and go out and live a normal life. What do you say?' The woman has her head buried in her bedclothes. I can make her look good. I make a few notes on the page in my clipboard and leave the ward. The nurse follows me and stops me in the corridor.

'Doctor. Do you really think plastic surgery is going to fix her?'

'Yes. In fact, nurse, I know so. There is a link between one's psychological state and one's physical appearance.'

'Doctor, with all due respect, she's been like that since she was fifteen years old. She lost her whole family in the fire that scarred her.'

'Well, it's no wonder she's mad then if she's reminded of her loss every time she looks in the mirror. I'll have her sane and out of this place by the end of the year. Mark my words.'

The nurse looks at me dubiously. 'Doctor?'

'Nurse, I'm a busy man.' I walk away from her.

'She lit the fire,' she calls down the corridor after me.

The next time I pay a visit to the ward, the vagrant woman is sitting by the window. I hardly recognise her. Her hair has been cut and she has been so thoroughly scrubbed that her skin shines like a child's. What I had held to be wrinkles the day she came in must have been grime. She is much younger than I had thought – she is not much more than twenty. She's wearing a white plastic wristband with the name 'Jane Smith' on it; she refuses to tell anyone her name or where she comes from or anything else about her. She is not of much use to me – except for that fact that she's not talking. I could perhaps use her for honing my skills in the finer points of surgery. The cosmetic kind. She's not ugly but I could certainly make her more beautiful. Good-looking people fare better in the world and it looks like she hasn't been faring very well.

Her palms are pressed against the windowpane and she has her face against the bars as if she wants to press it too against the cool glass. She traces the condensation with her fingertips. She twists her head sideways, looking up at the sky between tall buildings; at the same time, she rubs her bare feet on the linoleum floor, skin sticking and unsticking in jolts, as if she is trying to take flight.

'I'm Doctor Hargreaves. How are you today?'

She glances at me, then turns to the window again and makes a whining sound.

'I'd like to help you,' I say. 'You can trust me.'

She looks me right in the eye. She leans towards me and whispers something about rain but I can't make it out. Then she turns back to the window again.

I've decided to conduct a little experiment. Before leaving home in the morning I tear a handful of grass, still wet with dew, out of the garden and put it in a small plastic bag. It's been a week since I've been to the ward. I check on the burn lady. She is healing well beneath her bandages. Now I sit beside the Jane Smith. I have her hold out her hands and I shake the moist blades of grass into her palms. Her eyes widen and she immediately holds her cupped hands up to her nose and inhales deeply. With her eyes closed, she remains like that a long moment. Then she looks around cautiously and slips the grass into her dressing-gown pocket with her right hand and keeps her hand in the pocket; it expands and contracts as she feels the grass between her fingers. Her face lights up and is in fact quite pretty. 'Thank you, doctor,' she says.

I know what makes patients better and it's not always medicine or even surgery. Some patients shouldn't be patients at all. I watch her. She comes to life at the faintest whiff of fresh air – a gust of a draught that makes its way through door after door, along corridors and up stairs. She is not so simple or idiotic that she cannot get by in the world. I am sure of that. She can talk when she wants to.

Another week goes past and it's time to remove the bandages from the woman with the burns. I sit beside her bed, hold her hand and smile reassuringly. I peel the gauze strip from around her head and remove the dressing. I am so pleased with the result of my artistry I cannot help but beam at her. The swelling has gone down and there is still a lot of bruising but other than that she looks almost normal. I put a hand-held mirror face down on her lap. She takes a long time, but eventually she picks it up and looks at herself, sideways at first, in its glass. She touches the right side of her face, then she smiles a little. Then she smiles broadly at her own smile. She puts the mirror down and picks it back up, as if to double-check, like a child playing peek-a-boo.

On my way out I slip the patient who was a vagrant a daisy and whisper, 'I'm going to help you.' On my way home I stop at a department store. I buy a dress that looks like it will fit her. I also purchase a cardigan and a pair of women's lace-up shoes and some socks. I decide it is better to err on the side of too big with garment sizes.

I put the shoes and folded clothes on the seat of a wheelchair and put a blanket over them. When the ward is in its full hectic swing in the middle of the day and orderlies are bringing patients for their baths, I simply and deftly wheel her out of there. I take her down a floor in the lift and send her into a toilet with the bundle from under the blanket. She comes out in her new clothes, a little big on her but otherwise quite fetching.

She sits back in the wheelchair and I bring her to the ground floor, out past the reception to a garden area where those patients with mere physical ailments can be brought for a walk. The garden is dotted with people in pyjamas chatting to clothed relatives and friends, some walking around, some on benches, some in wheelchairs. They are all caught up in their own stories.

She breathes deeply. I motion to her to sit on a vacant bench. I sit beside her.

'Thank you, doctor,' she says.

'Henry,' I say.

'You are very kind, Henry.'

'I'm just doing my job,' I say. She takes off her shoes and socks and caresses the grass with her toes. I nod to an open gate, making sure her gaze follows mine. I place a purse of money on her lap. Then I stand up, wheel the empty chair around the side of the building and go in a different entrance to the one we came out of, leaving the young woman outside. I go to theatre to prepare for surgery.

We have experts now in the field of plastics who know all about how to mould or form useful objects that are also pleasing on the eye.

When Henry and Dolly woke up together in his bed the morning after the Surgeon Association's Christmas party, she had lost the brazenness she had as a hired entertainer the night before and he has lost his debonair affectations. She snuggled into his chest in half-sleep and he kissed her forehead. As she came to more and looked around, she turned her face away from him, slid out of bed, into her green dress and took her handbag into the bathroom.

After a few minutes of the sound of running water, Henry heared sobbing above it. He pulled on his boxers, went as far as the bathroom door, which was slightly ajar, and paused. He was torn between giving her privacy – after all they only just met the night before – and going in to see what's wrong. He said her name quietly, 'Dolores? Dolly?' He slowly pushed the door open to find her standing at the sink crying with the taps running.

'Are you okay?' he asked.

'No, don't look at me.' She turned away.

He couldn't help but go to her to comfort her. She tried to resist but he put his arms around her from behind.

'Shh. Shh. What's the matter?'

'I lost my make-up bag. It's not in my handbag.'

'What do you need that for? You're beautiful.'

'No, I'm not. I have to go.' She tried to get past him, but he embraced her firmly. He held her longer than he had ever held a woman he had brought home for a night. She needed to be held and not let go, he thought. As he continued hugging her, the tension left her body and she relaxed. He turned her around to face him and she leaned her damp face on his shoulder and wept some more. He led her back to the bedroom and lay down with her in his arms. As she drifted off to sleep, he whispered to her, 'It's okay, you're safe here. Just rest and don't worry about a thing.'

She'd caught his eye as soon as she walked into the ballroom the night before. She glided boldly through the crowd. Her dead-straight long red hair had a thick fringe that grazed the top of her long black lashes so that every blink resembled a butterfly closing its wings.

When he'd gone to talk to her he saw up close that her looks were mostly down to her height and make-up. Her face itself was doughy – something that could be moulded and puckered and pinched and pulled and tucked with nothing to lose. It was a blank canvas. Her body was slender, verging on boyish, a frame that could be built upon, filled in and filled out.

When she woke again, she was unafraid to look at him. He half sat up in bed and stroked her face. Her hair had begun to curl in places. One set of fake eyelashes was gone and the other still attached; smudged kohl made dark patches under her eyes. Henry gently peeled the remaining set of lashes from her left eye.

'I'm a mess,' she said.

'You're my perfect woman,' said Henry.

In the kitchen he made coffee and toast for them. She looked around at the modern decor and fittings. Everything was so fashionable in brown and orange. He even had an electric coffee-maker.

'You live here by yourself?' asked Dolly.

'Yes. My grandfather always told me not to get married until I was forty and well, I sort of ended up taking his advice whether I meant to or not.'

'You said last night that you're . . .'

'Forty.'

There was a silence between them for a moment. Then Henry cleared his throat and asked where she lived.

'In a big house in Camden, with some of the other people who were paid to be at the party last night. Artists, musicians, actors.'

'How many people live there?'

'I don't know. People just sort of come and go. No one really has their own room or anything.'

'And you're happy to live like that?'

She shrugged. 'It's better than being on the road on my own. They're like my family.'

'What age are you?'

'Nineteen.'

He paused and looked at her for a moment.

'You know you really are very pretty.'

'Stop it.' She looked down into her mug.

'I mean it. Come here.' He led her to a mirror on the wall. 'Look.'

'I don't want to.' She shook her head.

'Can you not see how beautiful you are?'

She looked in the mirror for a second, then away again. 'Leave me alone.'

'I see the beauty inside you, Dolly. And I want the rest of the world to see it too. I want you to be able to see it.' Looking into her eyes, he cradled her jaw in his hands and stroked her cheeks with his thumbs. 'Will you let me help you see it? Will you let me bring out the beauty in you?'

'Yes, Henry, I'd like that.'

The Lens

Our eyes let light in through the pupil and the lens helps create an image on the retina. Cameras are like eyes: they also have lenses and the shutter opens just long enough to let in light to form an image on the film. The chemicals on the film make the image permanent.

I prodded the photo in the developer tray with the wooden tongs, sent ripples over the emerging image. It was the one I took of Kristi the night before, doing stretches in the sitting room after her run, looking straight at the camera. She looked different somehow. There was a shadow around her head. Except it wasn't a shadow exactly; it was light in colour, more like a halo. Around her short dark hair was a very faint image of what looked like curls. A curly halo. Her face looked different, too. Her features seemed changed by shadows. Maybe I overexposed part of the picture. Or else it was the lighting. Maybe it was the new lens. But then a new lens – or rather an old second-hand one – couldn't change how Kristi looked in photos, could it? I hung the picture to dry and stood back. Was it the light?

I went into the kitchen and began making dinner. I put water on to boil for pasta. In another pot I made white sauce and while I stirred and it thickened, I couldn't stop thinking about the photo. I was still quiet with thought as I ladled out macaroni cheese onto plates half an hour later and Kristi and I sat down to eat.

'What do you want to do for your birthday, Fergus?' Kristi asked when we were halfway through dinner.

'I told you, nothing.'

'But thirty is a big one and it's next month. You have to do something for it.'

'No, I don't. Look, you know I'm not big into birthdays, so if I had a party it would be for other people not for me.'

'What's so bad about people wanting to celebrate your existence?'

'Nothing.'

'Oh.' Her tone changed like she suddenly understood something. She put down her fork and took my hand. 'Do you feel you're getting . . .? How are you feeling about turning thirty?'

'I'm not feeling anything.' Jesus, would she stop going on about it.

'Oh come on, Fergus, for once can you just open up and share what's going on with you?'

'I do share. What do you want from me, Kristi? Do you want me to make something up? It's only a birthday. I genuinely do not care.' I stood up and cleared my plate away. 'What's going on with me is that I want to go back into my darkroom to work on some prints.'

In the darkroom I took the photo of Kristi off the line and with a lens cloth buffed out any watermarks. It still looked weird. The shadow around her head looked almost like another person was in the photo with her, superimposed over her.

I picked up the camera. I turned and clicked the lens from its body and took off the cap. I checked the glass at both ends. Pristine. Like looking into a giant's eye. The weight of the lens felt good in my palm. It had definite substance. It was just shy of a foot in length and weighed 2.3kg. A Nikon 50–300mm, F4.5, made in 1971, two years before I was born. Things like this outlive their owners.

I held off on telling Kristi I'd bought the lens. We were saving up to visit her family in California, so anytime I bought something expensive she'd be hurt and think I didn't want to meet her parents. Of course I wanted to meet them – I mean we'd been together nearly three years and I'd definitely get some good photos out of a trip to the States. Another lens would be useful for the visit and would enable me to make more money to save for the flight by taking better photos.

With Kristi everything was easy and effortless from the start. Even us moving in together just sort of happened naturally. I was always staying over at her place, so when her housemate moved out I turned his room into a darkroom and started paying rent. The house was the gate lodge of an old mansion. Kristi had been renting it since shortly after she arrived in Ireland. She thought it was romantic that it was still standing while the big house was a ruin. She'd thought that the garden around it would be perfect for outdoor yoga. That was before she'd spent a winter here. Now it was overgrown with wild grass and nettles.

I bought the lens on eBay. It arrived in the post when Kristi was out at work. I put the receipt in the top drawer of my desk in the darkroom, then squashed the cardboard and bubble wrap and put them at the bottom of the bin round the back of the house.

She was wearing a tight, bright flowery dress the night we met at Fitzy's party. She was tanned and her short hair accentuated how pretty her face was. I'd fancied her straight away. She talked about beauty and feelings and stuff in that way Americans do. I found it endearing. She'd only just arrived and her accent was still thick – she hadn't yet developed that odd way of speaking a word or two per sentence in a Galway accent.

'Black isn't a colour,' she'd said to me when I told her about my work. 'It cuts you off from other people.'

'Really?'

'Yes, really. That's why religious orders and business people wear it. It creates a barrier between them and the world.'

'Is that so?' I smiled at her. Her confidence was arresting.

'Yes. That is so. So, why don't you take colour photos?'

'Well,' I said. 'Monochrome is more honest.'

'What do you mean?' She looked dubious.

'Black and white show the world for what it really is.' I walked out through the patio doors as I talked, away from the hub of the music and dancing, and sat on a bench. She followed, listening intently, and sat next to me, half-illuminated by the light falling through the kitchen window. 'You look at a scene . . .' I pointed to the chaotic dancing that was going on inside. 'And it is a complex mass of colours; then take a black and white shot of the same scene and it's simple. All the confusion is stripped away and you see it for what it is. The contrasts are obvious – it's just dark and light and nothing else.'

'Hm.' She furrowed her brow, looking at the window.

'And white . . . well, white is every colour of the spectrum all together, blended into their purest form. So . . .' I leaned closer to her and looked into her eyes. 'There is actually a secret rainbow of colours in every one of my black and white photos.' I fanned my fingers out to gesticulate the rainbow.

Kristi looked at me like I was the Dalai Lama and said in a breathy whisper, 'Wow, that is . . .' I went in for the kill. Truth was I didn't have the facilities in my darkroom to print colour. And the work I did for the agency was actually pretty much all printed in colour in their lab.

Agency work wasn't my art though. The real craft happens in the darkroom. The craft that takes time and patience and accuracy. The one where mistakes are expensive. It takes timing and know-how, where a speck of dust can ruin hours of work. I've always felt more comfortable in the darkroom than anywhere else. On my own in there with the door locked and nothing but the radio and the red light on I'm more content than I am in the company of most people.

The morning after she'd been trying to talk me into having a birthday party, I waited until she'd left for work before I packed my bag for the day's agency job – an agricultural show – camera, lenses, spare batteries, films. I made sure to bring my new lens. I'd originally bought it for moon shots but I thought it could also be perfect for candid portraits. The only portrait I'd taken with it so far was that one of Kristi, which came out distorted. The rest of the roll had been night landscapes.

When I was young it was my dream to work for *National Geographic*; to travel the world, scale mountains, cross deserts, icy landscapes, scuba-dive, see every bit of beauty the world has to offer, to document volcanoes erupting, turtle eggs hatching, cyclones whipping through the sky. I was going to throw myself at life. I wished I had the courage to pursue that dream, but easy jobs started coming in and I kept taking them and life just sort of happened to me.

When I'd trained as a photographer I got a few jobs for the local paper and joined an agency. I soon discovered that whether it was at a turning-of-the-sod ceremony, a charity raffle or a supermarket opening, the brief was always the same: whatever you're photographing, drape a pretty girl or two across it. That was my job.

Some organisers even hired models to be at events simply to look pretty. The opening of a hotel was the first time I came across this practice. The place was full of locals, wandering around with childlike curiosity and excitement, sipping free glasses of wine. Gliding through them were two girls a foot taller than everyone else, dressed up and made up like it was their graduation ball, hair lacquered into ornate shapes, faces hidden under masks of make-up. I was obliged by my job to ignore the local townspeople and to photograph these hired beauties instead.

It felt wrong so I took photos of ordinary people on a roll of my own black and white film. I knew there was no point in sending them into the agency, so I developed them myself. When I'd made a contact sheet, I put my eye to my magnifying lens and realised that I didn't need to travel the world for landscapes; they were right here, all around me. Landscapes abound with canyons, boulders, grasslands. Pores and wrinkles showed the humanity, just as crooked teeth did and nostril hair and sticky-out ears and double chins. I enlarged them and studied them. I printed details, close-ups of scars, chops, eyebrows, the curve of a cheekbone, the dimple of a chin. They spread on and on, an endless array of unique landscapes.

At the end of the agricultural show, when I had a few colour rolls of pretty girls and prized-cow photos to give to the agency, I put my new lens on and shot a roll of candid portraits of farmers tending to their animals, packing up, lifting pallets, opening and closing trailers.

When I got home, I got straight down to developing the film. I put it in the lightproof bag, zipped the bag up and slipped my hands into its gloves. With eyes closed to visualise what I was doing inside the bag, I transferred the film from cartridge to canister. Once it was sealed, I took the canister out and poured developer into it, put the lid on, turned it gently, counting the seconds, drained it then did the same with stop solution and fix, before rinsing it out under the tap. The front door opened and closed. Kristi was home from work. As I pulled the film out of the canister and hung it in the drying cupboard it curled like one of those fortune fish you get in Christmas crackers.

From the kitchen came the clatter of Kristi starting to make dinner. I loaded a new film and, from the doorway, took a few shots of her chopping vegetables for a curry.

'Stop it. You're annoying me,' she said. She turned towards the camera and narrowed her eyes. 'I've had a long day. I could do without your cyclops face now.' Usually when she called me that, it was in a joking tone, but she seemed genuinely bothered, so I put the camera down and set the table. Over dinner she talked about people from her work. I tried to listen, but

I'd never met her colleagues so it was hard to concentrate on following her stories. I nodded and looked out the window behind her, checking the cloud cover as twilight set in.

I cleared the dinner things to the sink while she got her gym gear ready. All the yoga and belly dancing she was into when we met were gone – all she did these days was run and do weights at the gym. Said she found it empowering. Once she was out the door, I abandoned the washing-up and went back to the darkroom. I needed to see how the shots taken with my new lens had come out.

We never had any photos on display at home when I was growing up. The walls were bare. All our school photos were put in a drawer and stayed there. When I was ten I learned how to make a pinhole camera from a children's science book. All I needed to make it was a tin can, some tissue paper and brown paper. When I put a blanket over my head and saw an upside-down image of a window on the tissue paper, I felt like I'd performed magic. By the time I was twelve I'd saved up enough money to buy myself a real camera. It was a Fujica Pocket 300 and took a 110 film.

I took the film from the drying cupboard, cut it into strips and placed them in rows in the contact printer. I locked the door, switched the red light on and the main light off.

Being in the darkroom is like being underwater. The tick of the clock is surreal. Fast and slow. I watch time passing and yet it seems to stand still. The hour hand is redundant. I'm only ever watching the second hand, counting thirty seconds to two minutes at a time, over and over with each print. Big time doesn't exist in here. Only small time.

I turned on the enlarger, raised and lowered its light to the right height. I turned the focus knob until the edges of the projected rows of negatives were sharp. I turned it off, placed a sheet of photographic paper underneath it and turned it back on. Counted the seconds, switched it off again. Lifted the sheet by its edges between careful fingertips and slid it into the tray of developer, poking it with wooden tongs to make sure it was evenly submerged. Watched the clock.

I picked the sheet out of the developer, placed it in the stop solution, watching the clock. Then into the fix solution, watching the clock. Then into the rinse tub with its steady trickle of fresh water flowing through it. I switched the light on, letting the world flood back in again, and went to make a mug of tea to distract myself from the impatient wait for the rinse.

When the contact sheet was dry, I laid it down and placed my loupe on the first frame, leaned my head down, right eye over it. I slid the magnifying glass over each tiny frame, one by one, and they enlarged under it. It was like looking into Lilliput. There, perfectly sharp and focused, appeared fully formed humans and landscapes, images from the agricultural show, like I'd caught them in a glass jar.

The images of the people were strangely different to what I thought I'd seen. I'd taken a few shots of a farmer hitching a trailer to a jeep. There was something odd about it. I printed one up in 8x10 so I could have a good look. There were shadows around his face that I couldn't account for. I remembered his face well, I thought, as I'd taken so many shots of him. Though he'd been clean-shaven, in the photo the shadows made the shape of a beard, a thick one like Brutus's from Popeye, but transparent – I could still see his face underneath it. I printed up the other shots of him. It was the same, no matter what angle I'd taken them from or where the light was coming from.

I heard the back door shut and ran out to the kitchen. Kristi was back already. It had got dark outside. She was scowling at the sink full of dirty dishes.

'Fergus . . .'

'I know. I'm sorry. I got carried away in the darkroom.' I filled the sink with hot water while she lit the fire. 'There's something weird going on with some of the photos I took today.'

'Yeah, like what?'

'Shadows and stuff. I'll have to show you.'

'All right. The gym was good by the way. Thanks.'

'Jesus, give me a chance to ask.'

She switched on the TV, sat on the couch then got back up again and put the kettle on.

'The house is freezing,' she said.

'I know a good way to warm up,' I said. She ignored the statement, filled a hot water bottle and lay on the couch again, wrapped in a duvet, watching some reality TV show. I sat in the armchair and watched her watching TV.

A portrait I took of her when we were first together hung above her on the wall behind the couch. None of my other work came close to it. In the background the grey grain of rocks, her hair wet from swimming in the sea, shining black like oil, her smile as loaded as a child's with joy, illuminated cheekbones, nose, chin, the contrast of lash after lash and the white dots of the catchlights in black pupils, like the last dab of carefully placed white an oil painter applies, tiny and brilliant, bringing the picture to life. When I'd found that reflected sunlight in her eyes, I pressed the shutter button with precision and carefully released again, knowing there was something significant in that moment I'd captured. Now I saw what it was: it was the look of someone in love. That was what was in her eyes when she looked at my cyclops face that day.

When the TV show she was watching was over she said goodnight, gave me a peck on the forehead and went to bed, dragging the duvet with her. I couldn't get the shadow pictures out of my mind. I went and looked at them again. The only thing to do, to see if it was the lens, was a controlled experiment.

'You're driving me nuts,' said Kristi as I followed her from the bedroom into the kitchen the next morning, clicking the shutter button. I took a few with my usual lens. Then I put on the new lens and took more as she lifted a box of muesli out of the cupboard. She looked at me with narrowed eyes, tutted and sliced a banana into a bowl.

I grabbed my tripod from the studio and set it up in the garden. Ran back inside.

'C'mon, Kristi. I need you for a minute. Honestly it'll only take a second.'

'But I'm having my breakfast. I gotta go to work in ten minutes.'

'C'mon!' I grabbed her arm a little more roughly than I intended.

'Ow!' She glared at me.

'Sorry. It's just . . . it's urgent.'

She followed me out to the garden, looking slightly worried. I beckoned her over to a patch of grass I'd marked with a stone.

'Here. Stand here,' I said. I ran to the camera, pressed the timer button and it began whirring its countdown. I ran to stand next to her and looked at the camera. She turned to me.

'What the fuck, Fergus? You dragged me away from my breakfast for a portrait with you? I have to go to work.' She walked away, shaking her head. The camera clicked. I got her in the frame. Side profile and pretty pissed-off looking, but she was in the frame.

'I know. I'm sorry. It's just I needed to make sure the shadows weren't from the house.'

Kristi stopped completely still – if only she'd stood that still for the photo – lowered her head and glowered at me from beneath raised eyebrows.

'I . . .' I began.

Then she turned and went inside, slamming the front door behind her, so I had to go around to the back. I slunk straight into the darkroom. She banged around in the kitchen for a while and then I heard the car revving and disappearing up the road.

I wasted the rest of the film so I could develop it straight away. The photos of her, taken with the old lens and the new one, were side by side on the contact sheet. In the ones taken with my usual lens she looked normal, her usual sallow healthy face and her dark cropped hair. There was a definite light area around her head in the ones taken by the new lens, a feathery halo of translucent blonde curls flicking back from her face. Her face was changed, too. Just slightly. Thinner, pointier features. And in the one of both of us, I have the shadow of a thick beard and my eyes look more sunken and closer together than they are. I brought the photos out into the daylight, laid them on the kitchen table, staring at them in turn. I needed to take more, to print more, but I was running low on film and had used my last sheet of photographic paper. I could pilfer some from work, but then I'd actually have to go to work, and I had more important things to do than that.

In the late afternoon I went out for a walk to clear my head. It was a pretty long walk; I went off-road through some fields and climbed over ditches to walk through other fields, taking mental note of good spots to return to for landscape shots. I must have been gone a couple of hours. Kristi was home from work when I got back and was watching TV. She seemed to have calmed down since the morning. I was ready to tell her. I wouldn't believe it myself unless I saw it, so I asked her to come into the kitchen and I showed her the photos I'd laid out on the kitchen table.

'See! That's why I needed you this morning.'

'Uhuh, a portrait of us,' she said flatly over my shoulder.

'No, look!' I pointed, making a knocking sound on the table with my fingertip. 'Look at your hair. And my face.'

'Yeah?'

'Look at the shadows on my face and the light around your head!'

'So you did some dodging and burning or whatever you call it.'

'No, I didn't. This is the way it came out. No tricks.'

'So it's probably a reflection or something.'

'It's not.'

'Okay, so is it possible there is some sort of a ghost image from, I don't know, the paper or the camera or the enlarger or something? You should know all that stuff, right?'

'Yeah, I just can't figure it out, though.'

'Right.' Kristi sighed.

I picked up one of the photos and stared at it. She stood up. 'Kristi, can you just take a few minutes to help me figure this out?' I said.

'Fergus,' she said. 'I thought we were going to the cinema tonight.'

'Oh shit. I totally forgot.' I put my hand to my forehead. 'I'm sorry. Can we still make it if we leave now?'

'No, it's too late. The movie starts in fifteen minutes.'

'I'm so sorry. Do you want go tomorrow night instead?'

'Tonight was the last night it was showing.'

'We'll have our own movie night,' I said, shuffling the photos into a pile and clearing them away. 'I'll go into town and get us a video and some munchies and a bottle of wine. I'll make popcorn.' She sighed and sat down at the table with her head in her hands, her shoulders slumping and her eyes welling up. I pretended not to notice her blinking back tears as I grabbed the car keys and my wallet.

Next morning I offered to drive her to work so I could wash her car for her during the day and collect her later. An apology for being so distracted lately. I loaded a colour film, as it was all I had, into my camera and brought it with me. Her workplace would be perfect for getting candid shots. The building is a huge metal cube in an industrial park of metal cubes. Galvanised blue walls, upstairs regularly spaced square windows all around it. Metal fire escape stairs on the outside. It's exactly the kind of place Kristi would have hated to work when we met. Back then she was happy with teaching a few yoga classes and a weekend job in a cool cafe. She kissed me goodbye and off she went, marching diligently in with all the other corporate workers to her customer support job. When she'd gone in, I sat in the car and aimed my camera at the door, my 1971 Nikon lens on it.

As people arrived, I took shots of them getting out of cars, pausing as they opened the door. I was a private detective on a case. Shutter click after shutter click, I collected people. I looked up – there was Kristi standing at a window in the first storey, looking straight down at me, shaking her head slowly. I put the camera down on the passenger seat and drove away.

In town I dropped the roll into the one-hour place to be developed. It was expensive but I needed these photos in a hurry. Sure enough, when I got them back, every man I'd taken a photo of had the suggestion of a beard and deep-set eyes and every woman the blonde bob and elfish face. But more than that, the colour had a yellow hue to it, as if the photos themselves were old.

I took out a chunk of my savings and bought a load of colour films. Every day, after I'd taken the work shots for the agency, and sometimes before, I shot a whole roll of strangers. Then I'd take it to the one-hour place to get it printed. I started driving to a different town every day, so I'd be taking photos of different people and going to different chemists to get them developed. I missed a lot of work and was running out of ailments to use as excuses. I got a warning from my boss.

Their faces became clearer and clearer with every new roll until there stared out at me completely different people to those I'd taken photos of. The man had big curly hair sticking out from behind his ears, a springy beard to match, and a receding hairline stretched his forehead all the way back to the top of his head. The woman had green almond-shaped eyes, a pinched nose and a wide smile. In the shots of her on her own her eyes have the look that Kristi's had in the swimming portrait. The ones of the man had no catchlights. Just dark eyes. No light, not even in the one of them both standing side by side, looking in the same direction; her eyes had catchlights and his did not.

The background started to change too. It was all green and blue. Grass, trees and a river. A fishing rod behind them, propped up with its line in the water. Another of him, holding a fish and smiling.

Eventually there were twenty-two photos of them and two of a bureau (which must have been taken to use up the roll). Pentimenti of photographs this lens had taken years ago. The pictures kept repeating themselves, every twenty-four frames, clearer every time. I printed out all the photos until eventually I had a bundle that I could have just dug out of someone's attic, they looked so genuinely from the seventies. She was wearing white flares, a turquoise-patterned shirt with huge lapels. He was in a mustard jumper and jeans so tight they were borderline indecent. The couple were hugging in one photo, kissing in another. There were several of him smiling and sitting on a little fishing stool, holding a rod.

I thought, if I take just one more set, I can get them even clearer.

'That's £6.99, please,' the woman in the chemist shop said, holding out the envelope of prints. I pulled my last tenner from my wallet.

Then again, maybe this was as clear as they would get.

When I got home I tidied the place up, dusted and hoovered the kitchen and sitting room. I lit the fire. I opened the cupboards to make dinner. It had been a few days since I'd cooked. She'd relax once I surprised her with . . . there wasn't much food there to make a meal. No potatoes. Not even enough pasta. Every cupboard was pretty empty. I supposed we hadn't been grocery shopping together in a while, but it wasn't like Kristi to let things run out.

When she came in from work, she sat down at the kitchen table and asked me to sit, too. Her face was stony.

'We need to talk,' she began.

'I know I've been a bit distracted lately and I haven't been completely there for you,' I said. 'But the photos . . .'

She let out a mixture of a sigh and a laugh.

'Remember that weird portrait of us a few weeks back? Well, look.' I handed her the latest bundle of photos. She took them and leafed through them.

'Who are these people?'

'I don't know who they are, but they are the only thing my new lens will produce photographs of.'

'New lens?'

'Wait,' I said, ran to the darkroom and grabbed the cardboard box of photos. There were hundreds of them now, chronologically ordered by when I had them printed.

Kristi took a deep breath and said, 'Listen, Fergus, I'm really sorry . . . but I need you to move out.'

'Just look.' I waved a handful of photos in front of her.

'I'm done, Fergus.'

'You could at least give me some say in this. Let's talk before making any big decisions.'

'Oh, now you want to talk.' There was snide sarcasm in her voice that shocked me. I wiped the table clean with my sleeved forearm and began spreading the pictures out on it in front of her.

'If you just let me show you these, you'll know what's been going on with me. I did tell you a few weeks back, but you didn't listen.'

'I'm sorry, Fergus. I love you but I can't live like this any more. I'll go and stay with Elaine for a few nights to give you a chance to pack your stuff.' She stood up.

'Who's Elaine?'

'My friend from work. I've told you about her. You know . . . oh forget it.'

'Wait . . .'

'Oh, and you never did wash my car that day.'

She picked up her gym bag and a suitcase I hadn't noticed until then and walked out.

When I heard her car leave the driveway, I shouted, 'Bitch!' I threw the chair she'd been sitting on after her, in the direction of the front door. I followed it into the sitting room where it had landed. I grabbed the front of the couch and flipped it onto its back and did the same with the armchair. I turned the coffee table upside down, breaking her favourite mug in the process. The burst of energy passed as quickly as it had swelled, and I was left shaking. I righted the furniture. I found a tube of superglue in one of the drawers in the sideboard. I picked up Kristi's mug and its cracked-off handle. I sat at the kitchen table and I glued it back together.

Then I felt the quietness. I'd always liked having the house to myself but there was suddenly a terrifying emptiness to it. A finality to the silence. I looked at the photos I had spread out, went to the fridge for a beer but there was none. I scrabbled around at the back of the cupboard in the sideboard, found a bottle of ouzo someone had brought us back from a holiday. I poured a glass of it and winced at the first taste. I knocked it back and poured another glass. I drank until the bottle was empty.

I woke freezing, my joints stiff with cold and my back aching from the uneven couch. It was dawn. My eyes stung and felt puffy. My head was pounding and my bladder was bursting. As I stood up, the framed portrait of Kristi fell from my arms and the glass cracked on the floor.

I was closer to the back door than the bathroom, so I went outside and pissed into the weeds, looking at the bin. I thought of how I'd hid the wrapping from the lens the day I received it; a realisation came to me that I was a small bit relieved that we were breaking up.

I took a couple of paracetamol and began gathering my things. I threw my clothes into black bags and my CDs in on top of them. I didn't own much else besides my photography equipment. I carried the enlarger and trays to the boot of the car and put all the smaller stuff in a box. In the darkroom I opened the top drawer, took out the eBay receipt for the Nikon lens and put it in my pocket. With the boot and back seat full, I put the box of photos on the passenger seat and placed the lens on top of them. I closed the front door of the gate lodge for the last time, then drove to the agency and collected my last pay cheque. I'd been fired in my absence for not turning up to jobs.

I cashed the cheque straight away and filled the car with petrol. Then I took the receipt for the lens out of my pocket. The sender's address was on it: Mr J Deane, 36 Cardigan Lane, Braintree, Essex. I stuck it on the dashboard and headed for the ferry port. I had no plan other than to deliver the photos but that somehow seemed a worthy enough cause to be alive that day. Maybe it was time to throw myself at life and see what would happen.

Coarse Fishing

Fishing is one of the UK's most popular hobbies. Not only is it a thrill to see and catch the fish, it is also very relaxing to witness wildlife on or around the water. Most anglers these days practise a philosophy of catch and release, returning all fish back to the water alive and unharmed.

The first part of Tegan that Nigel fell in love with was her tits. She was wearing a salmon-coloured polo-neck jumper and he was certain she was braless, as had recently become fashionable. She still had a solid body, even though she'd had a child. Thankfully the boy was away at his grandparents. Nigel wouldn't have to pretend to be interested in the little brat. It was warm in the house, an ugly little new build, the same as every other bungalow on the street, and he could make out the soft swell of Tegan's nipples, the subtle ring that marked their edges near the peak of those neat mounds under the ribbed polyester.

'What a fine spread,' he declared taking a seat opposite her. His eyes swept the table: beef pie, its crust flaky and golden, her tits, bowls of vegetables and potatoes, her tits. God, how he wanted to make those nipples hard, make them stand out like bullets.

Split shot are shotgun pellets that have slots cut halfway through them to make small weights. The slot allows them to be pinched onto the fishing line so that they sink the baited hook and make your float cock. The closer the bottom weight is to the hook, the more sensitive it is as a bite indicator, which you can see as movement in your cocked float.

'Thank you so much for inviting me over. It's not often a bachelor gets to enjoy such a feast.' He flapped his serviette out onto his lap.

'So, Nigel, how's running the supermarket going for you?' James's voice coming from his right startled him. He'd almost forgotten he was there.

'Very well, thank you, James. Of course, having a degree in business puts me at a great advantage.'

'Did you learn an awful lot at university, Nigel?' Tegan asked, immediately blushing. 'Sorry, that was a stupid question, wasn't it?'

'Not at all, Tegan. In fact, what I found more valuable than any of the book-learning was getting out of my hometown, living somewhere else, getting some life experience. But why am I telling you that? I'm sure you know what I mean?'

'Absolutely. That's why I left Wales.' She nodded vehemently, eyes wide.

'And came to Braintree, Essex! Ha!' He laughed.

'Yes, well I wanted to go to London but they transferred me here. I thought I'd be close enough to visit London sometimes.' She paused. 'And, anyway, I'd never have met my James if I hadn't moved here.' She reached across the table for James's flaccid hand; he looked uncomfortable.

'And have you taken her to London, James?'

James looked at Tegan. 'You never said you wanted to go there.'

'I'm sure I did.'

'I'm sure you didn't.'

Tegan turned to Nigel and said, 'There are so many things I would like to see in London. I read about the Whispering Gallery in St Paul's Cathedral. I don't know why but I've always been fascinated by the idea of it. You see, you whisper into the wall of the dome and your words circle all the way around and can be heard at the other side.'

'Fascinating,' said Nigel.

'You never mentioned that before,' said James.

In the ensuing silence Nigel considered all he had learned over the last few years. Women like men who are powerful. They like men who are intelligent and experienced, who are decisive and know what they want. They like men who notice things about them. He looked right at Tegan.

'Those earrings are very pretty, Tegan. They really bring out the colour in your eyes.'

Tegan touched a hand to her right lobe as she said thank you and averted her gaze to the table. He swore her nipples contracted just a little. He was stiff for her beneath the dining table. James half-choked half-coughed and dropped his fork on his plate. Nigel sat back with his hands behind his head.

84

It can be hard to hold your rod steady all of the time. A bank-stick is a metal pole with a screw thread at the top which allows a rod-rest to be attached. You can rest your rod on this while you stretch your arms and legs.

Nigel turned to James, smiling a toothy, hairy grin. 'Are you all right, pal? Tell me, how is work in the post office treating you?'

James gathered himself.

'Very well, thank you. In fact, I'm due a raise next year.'

'Really? That's nice,' said Nigel pouring more wine into Tegan's glass.

Remember to stay calm when you feel a bite. If you get too excited, you could lose control of your rod.

When he first started university, Nigel went with the other lads to the bars and nightclubs they went to. They stood around talking and drinking and wooing the girls. As he stood back and watched and couldn't help thinking analytically about the issue – he was, after all, studying business. There must be some easier, more time-efficient method for getting girls, and if not more time-efficient at least with a guaranteed return. So, one Saturday night, he dressed up in his smartest outfit, slicked and parted his hair and splashed extra aftershave on his cheeks. He locked his room and headed for the front door of his hall of residence.

'You not coming with us?' one of his mates called down the corridor. 'You got a hot date instead, have you? Hey, lads, Nige has a date!'

He slipped out of the door before he could suffer the full extent of their chummy jeering.

He got a bus to the other side of town. When he got there, he walked the streets until he saw some young-looking girls dressed up, talking and giggling about some dance they were going to. They passed around a bottle of cider, drinking as they walked.

'We'll never get drunk sharing this between us,' one of them whined.

'We'll just have to find a gentleman to buy us drinks then,' another said, wiggling her hips as she tottered on her heels. Nigel stroked the wallet in his pocket. He followed them, without seeming to, as if he just happened to be heading to the same place.

A hot spot is an area that seems to have fish all the time. Nevertheless, no matter how many fish appear to be available for the taking, a beginner angler needs to learn about the different species, as well as getting a good grasp of fish anatomy.

Inside, the dance hall was darker than the pubs and nightclubs he went to with his friends. The walls were papered in dark peeling patterns. A whiff of stale drink, smoke and vomit rose up from the sticky carpet. He went to the bar and watched the girls he'd followed. They stood at the other end of it, applying lipstick, adjusting their breasts and looking around them. He ordered himself a pint of pale ale. He strolled around the place. He guessed there was scarcely a person there over the age of eighteen. The place was already busy when he'd arrived, and couples were sitting at long benches and leaning against walls French-kissing. The band was out of tune and the dance floor full of boys jumping around and girls trying to teach them to jive. There was a back door open and he walked out through it to find couples ensconced in the shadows, between bins and in corners, black silhouettes of young men buried in shuffling, jiggling puffs of pink and yellow dresses.

He returned to the bar.

'Four halves of cider for those girls over there, please,' he shouted. The acned barman carried out the order with a scowl. He pointed to Nigel as he put the drinks on the counter and the girls giggled. They swayed their way over to him.

'Thank you for the drinks,' said one of them.

'You're welcome. It was the least I could do for the pleasure of seeing such beauty.'

They giggled again.

'I'm Nigel.'

'I'm Edith, this is Vera, Doreen and Ivy,' said Edith pointing to each girl in turn. 'We're very pleased to meet you, Nigel. You got any fags?'

Edith did most of the talking and all four of them had their drinks gone within minutes.

'Oh no, I'm empty,' said Edith looking at Nigel.

'How about you come outside with me for . . . a breath of fresh air . . . and I buy you girls another round?'

Edith smiled. Red lipstick streaked her teeth.

'That sounds like a plan, Nigel.' She hooked him by the arm. 'Get the drinks order in first.'

Two drinks later, Ivy went outside with him. And when he went back the next week Vera and Doreen took turns going outside with him.

'Bagging up' is a term used to describe an angler catching a large number of fish. Gudgeon is a species that it can be easy to

do this with as they are very greedy and stupid. When you find a shoal, they will stay around taking as much bait as you cast to them, no matter how many of them you catch.

As she rounded the end of the condiments and cereal aisle Tegan walked right into Nigel. She jumped and gave a little squeal.

When investigating close to the water's edge, always tread carefully. Any sudden movements or loud noises will scare the fish away.

'Careful there, young lady.' Nigel caught her gently by the elbows. She wore a flowery blouse, damned ruffles concealing her tits.

Tegan blushed.

'Sorry, Nigel. I didn't see you there.'

'I'm glad I bumped into you – or you bumped into me – I've been wanting to thank you for a wonderful dinner on Saturday.'

'Oh, it was nothing. I'm actually a bit embarrassed. I don't normally drink quite so much.'

'Oh nonsense. Your company was positively enchanting. It was nice to see you relax and enjoy yourself.'

'Well, I tell you, I had quite the headache on Sunday morning.'

'I had a touch of a hangover myself. But I always find getting out for a bit of fishing fixes that.'

'Really?'

'Yes, fishing seems to cure everything for me. It's the fresh air, the sound of the water lapping, the birds. I can switch off completely and yet I'm at the same time highly alert, waiting for signs of a bite.'

'That sounds fascinating. Perhaps getting out into nature would have fixed my headache, too. Next time I shall take my camera out for a walk.'

Why don't you come with me next time I go out fishing? No, not yet, Nigel. Wait. Let her think of it herself.

She paused, looking at him for a moment, as if thinking. Then she said, 'Well, I'd better get going.'

'Take care, Tegan.' He touched her lightly on the shoulder. He watched her arse as she walked away, white flared trousers hugging it tightly.

An attractant is something that an angler can add to their bait in order to attract fish into the swim.

'I seen you here before, 'aven't I? You friends with Edith and that lot, ain't ya?'

She was taller than Nigel, with blonde hair twisted up in a beehive and a red dress that displayed her melon-like tits, almost as far as the nipples. He could see where she had powdered the canyon of cleavage between them.

'Yes, I suppose I am. Can I buy you a drink?'

'Ooh that's very kind. I'll 'ave a crème de menthe, thank you.'

He handed her up the drink and was suddenly lost for words. How could he talk to this one? He hadn't been aiming this high.

'So, Nigel, ain't it? What do you do for a living, Nige?'

'I'm a student.'

'Oh, fancy that!' She laughed, knocked back her drink and handed him the empty glass. He nodded to the barman for another. And soon another. She talked and talked so that he could not get a word in.

'Me, I'm an actress,' she said. But she had to work as a waitress at the moment. Another drink. It's hard trying to make it in showbiz. Eventually, his wallet getting thin, he managed to suggest they go outside for some air. Fantastic idea she said, she just had to go to the little girls' room first to powder her nose. Powder her nose, my arse, Nigel thought, she'll be pissing like she's swallowed the incredible hulk after all that green stuff. He looked into the bottom of his own empty glass and adjusted his trousers. After a few minutes he looked up to see her come out of the toilets, a huge muscular man put his arm around her, and the two of them leave laughing. He never even got her name.

The wily roach can quite easily suck the innards out of bait. When fishing for them it's worthwhile inspecting your hook when you think you have a bite in case they have sucked the bait dry!

'Hey mister, want to buy us a drink?'

Two other girls were circling him, one either side. They were greasy-looking and they stood so close to him that their stale smell overpowered that of the carpet.

'No, I don't.' He looked straight ahead.

'Oh, go on. Be a gentleman.'

They buzzed around him like flies.

'Go away. No, forget it. I'm going home.'

He stormed out of the godforsaken place and headed towards the bus stop two streets away. When he went to pay his fare, he felt for his wallet but his pocket was empty.

The bleak and ruffe are two small fishes that are a source of annoyance to many anglers because they pilfer the bait meant for bigger fish.

Nigel sat looking out of the train window at the countryside as it rolled past. He'd got tired of the girls at the bars and dances. They were too silly, too derisive, too greedy. They were too much hard work. He had decided to take a different tack; he was going for wholesome girls, the outdoor type, instead. He would find them in quiet places, where he could pursue them undisturbed. He bought a rod and began making expeditions by himself.

It may seem obvious but locating the fish really is key to having a successful day on the bank. Fish are drawn to areas which offer them food and shelter and some of these locations are easier to find than others.

When he arrived at the rural station, he followed a path to the lake and then walked its perimeter until he found a suitable spot. He unpacked his gear, set up his stool, put his flask and sandwiches beside him, cast his line, put the rod in the rest and waited. He was nervous and so excited that his palms sweated, but he did his best to look like a placid angler. He had to make an effort to keep his eyes on the rod and not to keep looking down the path to see if anyone was coming his way. The odd sideways glance was enough.

Take advantage of any natural shelter such as bushes, trees or tall grass. Hide yourself behind or against them. Stay sitting low and prepare your tackle back from the water's edge.

Half an hour later a young blonde woman in tracksuit bottoms, T-shirt and running shoes came walking briskly along the path. She nodded hello as she passed.

'Excuse me,' Nigel called after her. He picked up the rod and made it look like he was straining.

'Yes?' The woman stopped.

'I've got a fish on my line here, so I can't let go of the rod. Would you mind passing me my net, please?' He nodded towards the net ten feet or so away, beside a bush. 'Silly me, I left it over there when I unpacked my things. And this is the first bite I've had all day!'

The woman smiled and walked towards the net, her back to Nigel.

Once they spot it, Perch tend to gorge on their prey without stopping to notice if there is any danger. Specimen size perch tend to hunt alone which makes them an interesting challenge.

Heart beating fast now, he could hardly believe his plan was working so well. He got up, put the rod down and moved towards her. She bent down, picked up the net and turned around more quickly than he expected. She saw him. Dropped the net.

'It got away,' Nigel said, still walking towards her.

'My husband is with me, he's just over there,' she said. 'He's waiting for me.' She walked quickly, then ran.

'Bumped off' is the act of losing a fish through the use of heavy tactics. They are usually lost due to the hook coming free of the mouth when sudden movements are made.

He hurriedly packed up his tackle, taking no care to put things in their right places. With his hat and sunglasses on, he went straight to the station and got the next train back home. That was the end of that fishing spot. He'd been so close. But no matter. He'd try somewhere new the next weekend. Variety is, after all, the spice of life.

Nigel's next fishing adventure took him two hours by train and then a bus journey and a long walk down a remote riverside. He went on a weekday this time because the great outdoors would be less busy. An older man walking his dog passed him and said hello, commented on the weather. Nigel responded without fully turning around, most of his face concealed by his hat. An hour passed before the next passers-by. A couple. They were deep in conversation and didn't acknowledge him, if they had even seen him. Then finally another two hours later, a woman on her own. He tried the line about the net again. He just had to be quicker this time. And he was.

Bream is a nomadic feeder. It tends to feed most on days that are overcast with a slight wind that ripples the water. Once caught, it seems to accept its fate and seldom puts up a struggle.

She looked older than he had thought she was from a distance. Her face was weathered, and she reeked like she hadn't washed in a long time. She was dressed in shapeless dark layers. Then he noticed her shopping bags, spilling out on the bank with what must have been her worldly possessions. Dirty rags of clothes, a filthy blanket, some plastic bits and pieces, a hospital wristband, a tin foil parcel.

'Do whatever you want. Just please don't kill me,' she said.

He looked at her, disgusted.

'I'm not worth killing,' she said.

Most coarse fish are rather unpalatable. That is why it is a good idea to return them to the water without damaging them. Bream in particular have a strong stench which means you will need to give your tackle a good wash after fishing for them. A stink bag is useful for carrying your nets.

'Go on, get out of here,' he said afterwards. She stood up, gathered her things back into her bags with leathery hands. She took her time; this unsettled him. She turned to him and looked right at him, expressionless. He was horrified by her looking at him. She was supposed to run away. He reached in his lunchbox, took out a sandwich and handed it to her.

'Here. Go,' he said.

She put it in her coat pocket, picked up her bags and walked away, stoop-headed. He knew she wouldn't tell anyone.

When a fish is 'gassed up' it has been brought to the surface from a great depth and cannot swim off after release. It is similar to a scuba diver getting 'the bends' from the change in pressure.

Nigel watched from behind the one-way mirror over the vegetable stall – from back here in his office he could observe his staff and customers. He watched Tegan walk down each aisle as if looking for someone around every corner. She patted her hair as she went and shifted the waistband of her mini-skirt. She looked directly at him as she checked her lipstick in the mirror, rubbing her lips together and puckering them towards him. He took some aftershave from his desk drawer and slapped it on his neck.

He stepped out onto the shop floor. She looked up, grabbed a turnip and surveyed it nonchalantly, with a shaking hand.

'Ah my favourite customer! Back so soon, eh? What did you forget to get this morning? Turnip, is it?'

'Oh, hello, Nigel. Yes, well, I just fancied something different for dinner.'

'Ah yes, variety is the spice of life.'

'Yes.' She stared at the turnip.

'You've been in so much lately I'm beginning to wonder if you're just coming to see me.' He grinned.

She turned beetroot. 'Well, now . . . I,' she stammered. He leaned down to her, put his hand on the turnip she was holding. She smelled clean and fruity and flowery all at once. Her top was tight today and it was cold in the vegetable aisle.

'Or maybe that's just wishful thinking.'

Because carp is one of the most sought-after coarse fish, there are many carp baits on the market, but you can find plenty of foods that will tempt carp in your local supermarket. Try luncheon meat, sweetcorn from a tin, or float the crust of a loaf of bread on the surface of the water.

Before she could say anything, he took the turnip from her and put it down.

'Come, my dear, you must try one of these strawberries.' He held one up for her in front of her mouth. 'Doesn't it look like it's ready to burst it's so ripe? Have a bite.'

She barely had to move her head to take a bite, and the juice left her lips wet. He took the remaining half into his own mouth, looking at her as he chewed. She licked her lips.

'You enjoy the finer things in life don't you, Tegan?'

'Well . . .'

'How is little Ben these days? Does he enjoy school?'

'Oh yes, he loves it. And I love having some time to myself to do the things I enjoy. I think I forgot who I was during the years he was very little.'

'How is your photography coming on? Not everyone around here would understand an artistic sensibility like yours, but I have a keen eye for detail. Comes from my fishing, you know. I'd love to see some of your work sometime.'

'Well, I've recently started taking portraits instead of landscapes. I prefer it.' She was comparing punnets of strawberries. 'Candid portraits, you know, of people doing what they do. But it can be difficult to find people to take photos of.' Her face flushed red again.

'Well, I'm available if you ever need a subject. I take no responsibility if my face breaks your lens though!'

She looked at him now. 'That would be a great help, thanks. Perhaps I could take some photos of you next time you go fishing? That is, if you don't mind me tagging along.'

'Rise' is the action of a fish coming to the surface to take the bait. When we 'play' a fish, we manoeuvre it in a give and take way before landing it.

Nigel led Tegan across stepping-stones to the other side of the river and through woodland to his secluded fishing spot on a small lake. It was off a tributary of the main river.

96

'No one else knows about this place,' he said. 'Does James know where you are?'

Tegan looked away. 'I told him I was going to a photography class, which is sort of true.'

'Yes, it is.'

'I mean I'm sure he wouldn't mind me meeting you. After all, there is nothing for him to worry about, so it's just easier not to worry him, you know?'

'Absolutely. He has nothing to worry about.'

A strong rod is needed for carp fishing. The hook must be completely hidden by the bait because carp are intelligent and cautious. Particle baits, which sink to the bottom and get lodged in debris, are a good way to attract carp into your swim. As they move from morsel to morsel, this grazing can help break down the inhibitions of even the shyest carp.

She set up her tripod a few feet away from Nigel as it approached sunset. The light was perfect, she said. The sun cast a warmth on the whole scene from across the river. The water was glassy and reflected the pink of the dusk sky. The long grasses cast shadows like brushstrokes in watercolours. She was wearing the tight-arsed flares tucked into wellington boots. Her top half was concealed by a duffel jacket.

'What do you want me to do?' Nigel asked.

'Nothing. Just be natural. Pretend I'm not here.'

Although fish feed throughout the day, they feed most confidently at dawn and at dusk. The half-light provided by the rising or setting sun provides them with more cover from predators.

He set up his equipment back from the water. Then he took out a blanket, paused for a moment, and left it folded beside his stool.

Assemble your rod, making sure to have greased the ferrules in advance. Examine your rod to make sure the rings are in a perfectly straight line from butt to tip.

He sat in silence and his face grew serene. The sun dropped lower. After a while, she took the camera off the tripod and moved closer to Nigel, shutter clicking from different angles. She got close, stood to his side.

Carp fishing takes patience. You must be able to remain still and silent for a long time. The smallest vibration from the bank or even a shadow moving over the water will spook them.

'Just move your head slightly towards the camera, but keep looking ahead,' she whispered to him. 'I can get wonderful catchlights.' He did as he was told, the lens, her body, just inches away.

'What are catchlights?'

She took the camera down. Turned her head towards the river.

'Look at my eyes. See, the way the sunlight is reflected as little bright dots?'

He leaned around in front of her. She turned her gaze to meet his, closed her eyes and parted her lips.

'To hand' is the act of catching fish so that when the rod is lifted, the fish swings directly to hand.

Nigel emerged from his tent at break of day. Camping out gave him the advantage of being at the right place early. He had become quite the accomplished angler and had made several good catches over the years since he'd taken to looking for girls here. He had honed his technique on each trip. He stood and pissed against a tree; the steam rising from his piss mingled with the dawn mist.

Everything was already set up and he was ready and waiting for a bite. As he considered his breakfast, he heard quick footsteps and panting. She was tall and slender. Fit. Running. He stayed out of sight until she was almost there, then he ran out from the side as if he hadn't seen her and bumped into her so hard she fell into the water.

When it is time to strike, lift your rod upwards in a firm, controlled manner.

'Oh God, I'm so sorry, are you all right?' He kneeled down and held out his hand for her. Shocked and disoriented, she took it. Then seeing he was wearing a balaclava, she let go and tried to swim away. He grabbed her by the hair.

Eels can be a pest as they can get a cast and line into a frightful tangle. The tighter you hold an eel, the harder it will fight. They are powerful and they wriggle, which means unhooking them can feel like a wrestling match.

Against the bank she got an arm free and pulled off his balaclava.

'Silly girl,' he said, shaking his head over her as she thrashed in the water. 'Silly, silly girl. What have you done?'

A 'priest' is a short wood or metal club used to dispatch a fish in a humane manner.

The supermarket was quiet early in the morning. Tegan walked in, took a deep breath and approached him by the meat counter.

'Nigel, we need to talk.'

'Ah, Tegan, good to see you. What can I do for you?'

'I'm pregnant.'

Nigel flinched. He whispered, 'Jesus, Tegan, not here.' Then in a loud voice, 'Well, you could choose from the usual luncheon meats, or we have just got in a new honey-glazed ham which is very nice in sandwiches. Would you like to try a sample?' Dropping his voice to a whisper again he said, 'Don't you think that's an issue you should be discussing with your husband?' He walked behind the unmanned counter and cut off a sliver of pink ham. Held it over the counter for her. She looked at it with furrowed brow.

'I'm telling him tonight.'

'Good, you probably should have told him first anyway. I don't see what this has to do with me.'

She pressed her hands against the glass display fridge, leaned up as close to him as she could.

'No, I'm telling him about us.' She turned away.

For anglers, fishing is prohibited during the 'close season' when most fish are either preparing for, recovering from or actually spawning. You may be unaware that beneath the riverbed tiny eggs are developing and hatching.

He came around to the front of the counter, took her by the elbow, led her to a shelf, and said loudly, 'Or perhaps you'd prefer our tinned products. They're always handy to have in the cupboard for surprise guests.' Then he whispered. 'Now, Tegan, let's not be too hasty about anything.'

'Nigel, we've been sneaking around for six months. I can't lie any more. You said you'd marry me if I left him. You said you'd look after me and Ben. Well, it's time.'

'Wait, Tegan, we need to discuss this.'

A woman in a headscarf and rollers walked past, looking at them with intrigue. 'Can I help you, madam?' said Nigel with a big managerial smile. 'No thank you,' she said, took a tin of sardines and walked slowly on with her basket.

Tegan stared at Nigel and shifted from foot to foot.

'Look, meet me at our spot by the lake at six o'clock,' said Nigel.

'All right.' She exhaled, and her shoulders dropped as she walked out.

Fish are slippery because there is a layer of slime covering their scales. It is important that you learn to hold your catch carefully and firmly.

Nigel got there well before Tegan. He wanted to be ready for any scenario. He brought his fishing gear, of course, the keep net, gloves, knife, nylon, a sack. He paced back and forth. She arrived looking even more determined than she had earlier on in the supermarket. He held out his arms to her and she softened in his embrace.

A 'keep net' is a big net that extends down into the water, in which anglers keep their live catch.

'Tegan, my beautiful, complicated Tegan.' He kissed the crown of her head.

'You told me. You told me you'd marry me. You told me you wanted to have children with me.' She looked up at him, half authoritative, half imploring.

'Yes, I do, I do. But what makes you think this is mine?'

'You know I haven't slept with him in months.'

'But, Tegan honey, I have a reputation to uphold. I can't be seen to have been carrying on with a married woman.'

'You have a reputation! I'm willing to leave my husband for you, to disrupt my son's life, to throw away any kind of respectability I had! I'm willing to do it because I love you. Who cares about the reputation of a damned supermarket manager?' She pulled away from him, out of his arms.

'Tegan, Tegan, I'm just saying maybe it doesn't have to be tonight that you tell him.'

'Oh, and how long would you like me to wait? Until I'm out to here? Or here?' She held a hand in front of her stomach. 'No, it has to be now. I have to give James that bit of respect.' As she said his name, her voice wavered and she began to sob, quietly at first, then breathlessly like a child. 'Oh, what have I done?' She turned her back on Nigel. He stood behind her and pulled on his gloves.

It is wise to bring with you all the bits and bobs of gear you might need. A cotton glove, for instance, will come in handy when you need to get a good grip on a slippery fish.

He took a length of nylon out of his pocket and whispered to her heaving back, 'Don't worry. Everything is going to be okay. Everything is going to be just fine.'

Nylon is difficult to tie tightly. It is therefore necessary for the angler to learn special types of strong, reliable knots such as the stop knot, the double-blood knot, and the spade-end knot.

From behind, he covered her mouth and nose with one hand to smother the sound of her sobbing. He wanted to stop what he was doing but he couldn't. There was no other way. As he pulled on the nylon he began to cry himself.

'Shh. Shh. It's all going to be okay.'

He pulled the nylon tighter. He got her to the ground and slid her towards the water's edge.

If you are going to kill a fish, you must handle it carefully to reduce stress and kill it as soon as possible after capture. Never leave it to gasp its life away – this would be inhumane.

'My beautiful Tegan. I love you so much.' He put his hand on her face and pushed it gently under. Her hair spread out around her like blonde algae. The rippling water distorted her face, so it did not look like her any more. Her body twisted and floundered and thrashed and flailed and eventually, it slumped. He took his knife from his pocket, unfolded the blade from the wooden handle and cut off a long lock of her hair. He knotted it and put it in his tackle box.

Following these simple instructions will help you become a successful angler.

A Guide to the Stars

Craig sat on his bed and pulled from his wallet the pension money he'd collected earlier. He counted out most of the notes into a little pile and put the rest back in his wallet. He pulled the drawer all the way out of his bedside table and reached into the cavity behind it. The jar he took out was already stuffed with a thick roll of cash, but he managed to roll up the notes from this week's pension and slide them into the core of the cylinder. He lidded the jar, put it back into the cavity and replaced the drawer. On top of the bedside table was a tattered, well-worn book titled *A Guide to the Stars.* The walls of his room were still decorated with drawings he'd done as a child, over fifty years ago, of star constellations and of the moon.

The door to his parents' room was open. He'd left everything as it was after his mother died fifteen years before. She had left all his father's things as they were when he died twenty years before that. A stranger coming into the house would think there were three people living there. He'd thought about selling up, leaving Glasgow and moving to the island where his grandfather had lived, but he was set in his ways now and moving would be an expense. He went downstairs and made a simple dinner from reduced-price pork chops he'd got from the supermarket, boiled potatoes and some value-range tinned vegetables.

He was used to the quiet in the house during the day, but by the evening he sometimes liked to go somewhere with a bit of life. After dinner, he put on his coat and boots and walked to the Anchor Tavern, the only bar he'd ever really frequented. The quarter moon was waxing. He stopped for a moment to look at it and cast his mind back to the night man landed on the moon.

He'd been nineteen at the time. 20 July 1969. He'd listened to it on the wireless with his parents. It was a Sunday. His stomach had been in an ever-tightening knot for days beforehand. While he listened to the broadcast he kept forgetting to breathe. He felt as if it was being broadcast especially for him. One day he himself would go into space just like Neil Armstrong. He'd already been saving his money for the voyage since he started work in the shipyard at fifteen. Even before that he saved his pocket money and birthday money for it. He'd tried so hard to marry the moon he could see out of the window with the one that men had just landed on. He went outside to look at it with his binoculars. It was in its first quarter. He wanted to see the spaceship, see them walking on the surface, bounding around up there in their marshmallow suits. But all he saw was the usual face in the moon.

The Anchor was near the shipyard where he'd worked all his life until retirement, as his father had done before him. The barman nodded hello to Craig who took a stool at the counter and looked around. The Anchor was little more than a drinking hole. There was nothing ornamental about it. Everything in it was functional and durable enough to have survived past brawls. Bare dark wooden walls, a few tables, a big bleak bar with stools and that was all. There were ten or so people dotted around. None of the men who'd worked at the yard during his time were there. Not that he'd have anything to say to them anyway; he'd learned to be gruff to survive and had always kept to himself. He ordered a can of beer and poured it into a glass. He sipped at it.

When he was thirty-nine he read something in the paper that made him certain his time had come to go into space. He had by then borrowed every book to do with space travel from the library and read them from cover to cover. Naming the constellations was as natural to him as spelling his own name since his grandfather taught him all about them when he was a child. He knew he could never be a real astronaut. That was obvious even to him. He'd video-recorded an episode of *Tomorrow's World* in which experts predicted that by the year 2000 families would be travelling to the moon on their holidays, staying in lunar hotels. He'd watched it over and over again.

The smell of his mother's apple crumble came from the oven that Sunday afternoon as he sat at the kitchen table with the paper. He turned to a page that said *Astronauts wanted. No experience necessary.* It was an ad looking for the first British person to go into space. Anyone could apply. His breaths became deep and fast with his heartbeat. He stared at the ad, read it over and over, looking for the catch, but there was none. Fifteen minutes later he was at the postbox, sending off for the application form.

It arrived five days later. He spent every evening for a week working on it in his bedroom, checking and double-checking his spelling. In his personal statement he noted his extensive knowledge of the night sky and space exploration. He wrote that there was a family history of exploration and voyages through his grandfather's merchant navy service. He put into words the sense of destiny he felt about going into space. After he posted the application, he daydreamed about sitting in the payload, a crackling voice counting down to take-off. He had still never left Scotland unlike some of the young men in the yard. They went off to America and Australia and came back with all sorts of stories. The excitement with which they spoke reminded him of his grandfather and his tales, though their stories were more to do with how easy it was to get laid abroad by singing that Proclaimers song about walking 500 miles than they were about life-threatening situations. They had seen part of the world, but he was going to see the whole world in one go.

Three weeks and four days after sending off his application a letter arrived from Project Juno. He lifted it casually from the hall table where his mother had left it and took it upstairs, his steps measured and slow. He placed it on his bed, sat back and looked at it. He took a few deep breaths, savouring the moment his life was about to change. He picked up the envelope again, studied the Project Juno stamp on the top left corner in navy ink and ran his fingers over the surface of the paper. He turned it around and gently ripped it open. It was short. *Dear Mr Wilson, thank you for applying to participate in Project Juno. I regret to inform you that your application was unsuccessful.*

He wrote to them asking for another chance to apply, saying maybe there was more he could put into his application that he hadn't put in the first one. They wrote back thanking him for his enthusiasm and stating that they had already chosen their candidates. They could not enter into any further correspondence with unsuccessful applicants.

Every day he checked the papers and listened to the radio to hear news about Juno, even though any coverage of it made him feel feverish and nauseous. The four candidates were a navy physician, an army air corps major, a university lecturer and a woman – a food technologist – ten years his junior. They all went to Star City in Russia to train. In the end they picked the food technologist to go into space. He wondered if she'd ever even considered going into space until she saw the ad. Had she applied on a whim? After eighteen months' training, on 18 May 1991, she left Earth for eight days. Most of that time she was on Mir. She took photographs of the British Isles, performed medical and agricultural tests and communicated with British schoolchildren over amateur radio hook-up. All of these were things that Craig could have done. But when the day came on which you could buy a ticket for a space shuttle to the moon as if for a ferry to another country, he'd be ready. His money jars were filling.

Two young men came in and sat one stool away from him at the bar. They ordered beers and talked about a Celtic match. Craig half-listened in on their conversation but having no interest in football, he didn't know any of the players they were talking about. They were disagreeing about what the score had been. The one closest to Craig pulled out his phone and looked up the results. The dispute settled, they sat in silence as the young man continued to scroll for a few minutes.

'Jesus,' the one with the phone said. 'Stellar are doing commercial flights into space now.'

'You're kidding me,' said the other one.

'No, seriously, look.' The first one held his phone out and they both hunched over it.

'Ah shit, the girlfriend will be wanting to go there now on her holidays instead of the Canaries.'

'Well, it is that bit closer to the sun.'

Craig leaned over towards the two men. 'Excuse me, I couldn't help overhearing,' he said. 'What's that about flights into space?'

The young man swung in his direction and held the phone out for him to look at the screen.

'Here, look. Stellar Intergalactic Flights.' Craig's grandfather had been right all along.

'Are you thinking of a holiday in space yourself?'

Craig studied the screen and smiled. 'Aye, that I am,' he said.

The two men laughed. The one closest to him put down his phone and held up his glass. 'To old-timers in space!'

Craig raised his glass and the three of them drank to space travel.

The two young men soon fell back into conversation about football and Craig sat with a trembling hand on his glass, staring at the counter. The years of waiting and saving were about to come to an end. None of it had been in vain. He could let go of the regret he'd felt about Honey. He had made the right decision.

He'd met Honey here in the Anchor, which was a very unlikely thing as women didn't go in there very often and even less so in the early seventies. The Anchor was a place for working men. But there she was one night asking the barman where the jukebox was. He didn't know if she didn't notice or if she didn't care that this was not a place for pretty little rich girls. She had a few friends with her and they danced even though there was no music. Her long blonde hair and tie-dye skirt swirled around her. Her eyes were closed and she was smiling. When she opened her eyes, she caught Craig looking at her. She walked over to him.

'Hi,' she said.

'Hello,' said Craig, feeling self-conscious.

'Do you want to come to a party?' she asked in an Irish accent.

She grabbed a colleague of Craig's, Jimmy, and took him along to the party, too. Maybe she'd thought they were friends because they were standing next to each other at the bar. When, on the walk to the party, they told her they were ship-builders, she told them she'd had a ship herself, but it sank on its maiden voyage. She was laughing to herself. 'It was a Morris Marina, ha, Marina!'

'Isn't that a car?' asked Jimmy.

'I suppose the wheels should have given it away,' she said. 'Well, it rests in peace now anyway at the bottom of the harbour.'

Craig wondered what she was talking about but kept quiet.

The party was in a flat, filled with hippies like her. The sitting room was lit with candles and incense wafted in the air. There

110

was some music with a lot of flute in it on the record player and people swayed and made continually changing shapes with their arms in the air. Someone handed him a joint. He'd never smoked pot, never been around it before. He took a couple of drags and tried to hand it back to the person who gave it to him, but they waved at him to pass it on. He handed it to Honey.

'Do you like Bowie?' Honey asked Craig.

His face lit up and he nodded.

She crossed the room, lifted the needle from the record that was playing and put on 'Space Oddity'. She took Craig by the hand and led him away from the wall, into the centre of the crowded room to dance. He came to life as he sang along to every word as did most of the people there. He was high.

A girl took her top off and danced in nothing but a pair of bell-bottomed jeans. Honey took her top off too. Craig looked around and saw that Jimmy was the only other person there who looked as shocked as he was by the sight of their bare breasts. He was mesmerised. Honey looked at Craig as he watched her dance. Then she took him and Jimmy by the hands and led them both to her bedroom.

Craig spent all his free time with Honey after that first night. They spent a lot of time at her place. Her flatmates had all gone back to Ireland. Instead of saving his wages Craig spent them on drinks and dinners for the two of them. She'd told him right from the start that she thought it was okay to sleep with other people. It sounded like a good deal to him at first, except that for him there were no other women. 'The times are changing,' she'd said.

When they'd known each other a couple of weeks he decided to take her to the island. He always felt nostalgic for the place in the summer and he hadn't been back since his grandfather died when he was thirteen. It was late July and there would be plenty of shooting stars to see. He dipped into his savings and bought a tent and sleeping bags, so they could camp there for the night. He paid for the boat over.

She looked good in her poncho, sitting on the beach by the campfire. He stoked it with a stick; sparks flew.

'You're different out here,' she said. Her face seemed innocent and childlike in the glow. She hadn't any of her face paint on and looked natural.

'What do you mean?'

'You're more . . . well, it's like you're less on guard. You know?'

'Well, you're different, too,' Craig said.

'How?'

'You're less hippyish.'

'Oh no! Don't tell the others! Truth is I'm really just a good girl looking for a man to settle down with, so I can lead a wholesome life.'

'I don't even know if you're joking or not.'

She laughed. 'Well, this "not very hippyish" girl has brought along a little treat.' She took an envelope from her bag. He leaned in to look. She smiled and tipped two tiny squares of paper out into her palm. Holding one out on her fingertip, she gently prised apart his lips and stuck the paper on his tongue. Then she placed the other one in her own mouth.

'Now what?' he asked.

'Now, sit back and enjoy.'

112

He lay on the blanket and she lay next to him. He pulled her close. Then pointed. 'Cassiopeia,' he said.

'What?'

'That constellation there.' He pointed and drew lines with his finger in the air.

'Wow, most people only know the Plough. I only know the Plough. It's that one there, right?'

'No, it's that one over there.'

'Okay I don't even know the Plough. How do you know all this? Or are you just making it up to impress me?'

'My grandfather taught me.' He told her how he used to spend his summers on the island, leaving out the part about the medals.

His arms began to tingle and his legs a little too, and the stars grew brighter and began to waver and when he looked at Honey he felt uncomfortable and nauseous and wanted the wobbling eyesight to stop, but she smiled. As if reading his mind she said relax, give it a few minutes and he turned his head to look at the stars again and they glowed brighter and brighter and were closer to him and it seemed like he had only ever seen them in 2D and now he was seeing them in every dimension, really seeing them, and they flickered and glowed like organisms, like they had something to tell him and they all went on for ever and ever and the moon was brighter than ever and every speck on its surface was so clear, so close he could almost touch them. He took out his binoculars and he could see the valleys, the seas, the cliffs, all the surfaces on the moon, and he knew there and then he would go into space in his lifetime. If they could put a man up there, they could put any man up there, including him. He exchanged a sort of acknowledgement with the cosmos that it was his destiny to one day look back at Earth from space.

They lay on the sand for hours. Honey sat up and talked and watched the fire and urged him to look at it too, at its dancing flames and she got up and danced around in her poncho and now and then her slowly swirling figure cut across his field of vision as if she too were a part of the night sky. 'You're a comet,' he said, and she giggled, and her giggles left a trail of colours that followed her.

Two weeks into August she invited him around to her flat and cooked him dinner, something she had never done before. When they had finished, she looked at him with a nervous smile.

'Craig, we need to get married.'

Craig laughed. Honey didn't.

'You're serious?'

'I'm pregnant.'

As Craig looked at her, he suddenly realised how much money he'd spent on this girl already and now she wanted him to throw away everything to keep her and raise God knows whose child. She turned into a black hole in his eyes into which his savings had been disappearing since he'd met her.

'You've been sleeping with other men.'

'I know the baby is yours. I can feel it.'

'But you can't be sure it is.'

She looked desperate and indignant. 'You should be glad I'm willing to let you marry me. I'm completely out of your league.'

'Honey, this is not my problem. Maybe you can try Jimmy. I know for certain you were with him that first night we were together. I was there, remember?'

114

'But I love you, Craig.'

'I don't think you do.'

She started to cry.

He picked up his jacket and left the flat then, for the last time. He wasn't about to abandon his plans of space travel for a mess like that. He wasn't about to abandon his plans of going into space for anything or anyone. That's what he told himself, but the thought of her plagued him with guilt for a long time afterwards, and though it faded with time, he sometimes wondered what became of her and if there was a child somewhere who looked like him. She disappeared as suddenly as she'd appeared. He could never even look her up; he never got her surname. Or her first name for that matter – Honey was a made-up one she'd given herself.

Craig drained his glass and stood to leave. He nodded goodbye to the two young men at the bar and they nodded back. 'Bon voyage,' one of them said.

He walked all the way into the centre of town to a twenty-four-hour internet cafe. He signed in at the counter and sat at a computer. 'Stellar Intergalactic', he typed into the search engine. And there it was: a futuristic-looking website in the colours of space itself, declaring its mission to democratise space, to open it up to the ordinary person.

'Only 547 people have been to space,' the website read. 'Now Stellar Intergalactic is opening space to the rest of us.' He smiled as he read on. 'Because government space agencies are not asked to help ordinary citizens to become astronauts, most of our planet's seven billion people have had no opportunity to experience space and all of its possibilities for themselves, regardless of their passion or talent.'

He filled out the future astronaut registration form. He took his time with the section titled 'Your motivation for going into space'. For this he closed his eyes, breathed deeply and let all his feelings and memories around his ambition rise. He remembered when he first considered going into space as a real possibility. It was when he was staying with his grandfather the summer he was nine years old.

He remembered sitting with Granda Davie on the end of the pier at the tail end of twilight. The moon was coming up over the sea and the first stars punctured the growing darkness. It was hours past Craig's usual bedtime but Granda never gave him a curfew when he stayed with him on the island. Back home in Glasgow, Craig was never allowed outside at night, but during the summer months it was just him and his grandfather, the two lads together in the seaside house. During the day his grandfather took him fishing in his punt, got him to help carry out repairs to the house and the boat, they climbed rocks and explored caves and at night they played cards and Granda Davie told stories. Craig's gangly legs dangled over the water beside his grandfather's strong tree-like ones.

'Tell me about the time you were in battle at sea,' said Craig. The battle was one of Craig's favourite stories. He loved listening to his grandfather's voice; it was soothing, and his stories were exhilarating.

'It was a real war, Craig. None of your games with tin soldiers. I saw men die in front of me. I saw a shipmate's head roll past me on the deck that day.' His grandfather censored nothing and could string a story out for a whole evening. Sometimes Craig had nightmares after hearing them but never dared tell his grandfather that lest he'd think him less of a man and deprive him of future stories.

'We were in the middle of the Atlantic and I was on watch with my mate Tom when we got word that the Germans were approaching . . .' Craig watched Granda Davie while he talked. He was a big, gnarled man. His forehead reminded Craig of the way the sand formed ripples on the beach, thick smooth bumps and grooves.

'The best times were before the war though, Craig. Oh, the beautiful countries we saw.'

'I'd love to go on voyages like you did and see the whole world.'

'A sailor's life isn't a life I'd want for you, Craig. Especially if war broke out.'

Craig's heart sank.

Granda Davie looked up at the moon. You know,' he said, 'why not think bigger than that?' He put a hand on Craig's back. 'One day they're going to put a man up there on the moon. And I bet you by the time you're a grown-up, going to the moon will be just like going to another country.'

'Really?' asked Craig.

'Oh yes, I've no doubt about it. I bet you'll go on a voyage in a spaceship someday, Craig.'

That night Craig didn't have any nightmares. He barely slept at all with the excitement of thinking about how some day he was going into space. He didn't just think it though; he felt it.

The next evening, as the sun was setting, they were sitting at the kitchen table after a game of rummy. Craig's grandfather

117

stood, reached his hands up to the top of the sideboard, took down a biscuit tin and sat down again.

'I'm not going to live for ever, Craig,' he said. Craig didn't believe him, but at the words he felt a strange twinge in his stomach that he could not explain. He remained silent, looking up at his grandfather whose face now conveyed that there was a sense of solemnity about the evening. Granda Davie slowly took the lid from the tin and one by one took out medals, some with ribbons and pins.

'These are the medals I earned in the merchant navy, Craig. I'm not going to have a use for them when I'm gone, and no one knows as much about my navy days as you do.'

'What about Mum and Uncle Hugh?'

'No, I never told them anything. They were too young. I couldn't have them knowing what war was really like. No, Craig, you are the only one who knows what these medals mean.'

Craig sat up, a few inches taller with pride and importance.

'I want you to have these,' said Granda Davie.

Craig reached his hand across the table, only for his grandfather to push it away.

'But medals have to be earned, Craig.'

Craig nodded. Of course, he couldn't just be given them.

'So, I'm going to give you some things to learn and for every task you complete you'll get a medal.'

Craig nodded.

His grandfather stood up and beckoned him to follow.

'Come on outside.'

Craig followed him out into the garden. The cold dewy grass kissed his bare calves and the evening air chilled through his T-shirt. If he was back home, he'd be in pyjamas by now, not still in shorts and T-shirt.

'Now, Craig,' Granda Davie said, his head turned upwards so all Craig could see of his face was the silhouette of his chin, 'can you tell me which one the North Star is?'

Craig looked up and felt dizzy at the sight of the stars multiplying above him in all directions, further and further. Mouth open, he shook his head.

'When you're out at sea at night the ocean and the sky is all you can see. If you get into trouble you need to know where you are by looking at the stars.' He knelt down beside Craig and pointed upwards. 'See that bright one there? That's the North Star. Those three over there in a line? That's the constellation Cepheus.' They went back inside, and his grandfather handed him a torch and a book called *A Guide to the Stars* with all the names of the stars and constellations and pictures of them.

For the rest of that summer, Craig spent time every night outside lying on a blanket with the book, his torch and a pair of binoculars. Before the end of August, he was able to name every planet and every constellation in the northern hemisphere and his grandfather awarded him his first medal.

He learned the winter constellations as well, when he was back at home in Glasgow, lying out on the flat part of the roof above the bathroom when he was supposed to be in bed. Most of them he couldn't see because of the city lights but he worked with what he could see and imagined the rest. In school he'd often been so tired he'd slept in his classes. One of his classmates once called him a space cadet and he'd smiled at what was supposed to be an insult. Then they went back to calling him a weirdo.

Summers after that he learned to tie knots and the meanings of semaphore flags, but none of those tasks compared to his first one of learning about the night sky and that first medal. And he always dreamed of how different the stars would look when he was out in space looking back at the Earth.

Having filled out the form, Craig knew this time his dream was becoming a reality. The application wasn't looking for fancy qualifications or superhumans. They just wanted passion and diversity. And a $250,000 deposit.

His registration was processed, and he was invited to become part of the Stellar Intergalactic family. The day of his sixty-seventh birthday he emptied all his jars and counted out his money. Then he put the rolled-up notes into a duffel bag and went to the bank where he paid the deposit to go into space.

Ensemble

Cari opened her eyes. Her tongue was like leather and there was an ache in her bladder. Ben lay beside her, his nearly snore deep and measured beneath the duvet's rise and fall. She knew that the best thing to do was to get up immediately and start the day, wash the dream away with a shower. But instead she pressed snooze and lay there with eyes closed and tried to re-enter the dream, but the magic of it was gone. She pressed snooze again. Thoughts formed a puddle around her, crystallising into anxiety that would encase her for the day. It would crackle with every movement and sometimes she felt like she would disintegrate at any moment.

Most of the time she was content. Most of the time she loved Ben.

No time for a shower now and no time to walk to work. She rang for a taxi, washed the smudged make-up from her eyes and quickly dressed. When she got in the car, she realised it was the same driver who'd brought them home from the party only a few hours before.

She sat at her desk trying to figure out a way to take a nap, but the phone was already ringing. There were emails to answer. Payrolls to be processed. In a fog somewhere between drunk and hungover she managed to get through to lunchtime when she locked herself in the toilet and took a nap sitting there, head back against the wall. She could still taste Chris Jones's kiss from the dream.

She was fifteen when she went out with him. They'd both been in the school orchestra. His hair was black, straight, shoulder-length. While teachers sent any boy whose hair came to his collar to the hairdressers, they never bothered with Chris. Maybe because he was quiet and his hair length was not an act of rebellion. It was his quietness that had attracted her. His mystery. When she realised that behind his mysterious quietness was just a nice boy who was nice to her, she'd dumped him.

After lunch she searched for and found him on Myspace. His hair was down to his waist now, as hers had been until she'd cut it up into a bob a few years ago, and he had a full beard. He was in a metal band that had made it big in Finland. This was the first time she'd dreamed about Chris. The dreams were more frequent now and rarely about the same guy. Just always about a life in which she wasn't with Ben.

In the afternoon, sitting staring at a spreadsheet, she tried to remind herself of the good days with Ben, the early days – it wasn't just the early days, though. It was until about three years ago. That's when he started to cut her off. Until then she hadn't minded him lying around during the day because at least she had access to his every thought and feeling and he had always been loving towards her. Back then, they knew each other better than they knew themselves sometimes. Back then, they went to every party and were the life and soul of it, back then, they had their own code of looks they'd exchange across dance floors and bars and parties that made them invincible. They made such a cool couple. Everyone said so. Now though, he barely communicated with her at all. He could sit in sullen silence for entire days and he created an unbearable tension in their flat, even more so when she tried to be cheerful.

Ben woke up alone, again, with a headache, again. The light coming through the curtain had the muted shadowiness of a winter's afternoon. He pulled on his blue fleece dressing gown, went downstairs and made coffee. Things would be better after coffee, he thought. He sat on the couch, switched on the TV to the news. He lit a cigarette. After the news he watched a game show and after that a talk show aimed at housewives; when he looked at the time an hour and a half had passed. He got himself another cup of coffee. He lit another cigarette. He was bored. Bored of it all. Bored of the cold. Bored of being alone. He was hungry, too. He wanted to go into town, but he didn't have the energy. And he couldn't deal with daytime people anyway. He didn't want to have to stop and chat with anyone. By the time he drained his second mug of coffee, daylight was fading. Fuck, he said aloud. Another day gone by and he hadn't even been up to see any of it. Again.

He was starving by the time Cari came home. 'Jesus, you're not even dressed,' were the first words she said to him. She hadn't brought home any groceries. He said he was sick. She doesn't understand, he thought. She's cold and unfeeling. If she really cared about me, she would know something was wrong and she'd look after me. She would show some empathy. She looked haggard and pale without her make-up.

There were lines on her face and bags under her eyes and lately her jaw wasn't the sharp line it used to be.

It was three years since he'd found out about his mother. Of course he was going to tell Cari. He was going to tell her right away. But when she came home from work that day, the day he'd got the phone call from his father, she was cranky, so he waited for the right time to tell her. When is the right time to tell someone that your mother's body has been found? Over dinner didn't seem appropriate so he waited until afterwards. Then he thought maybe he'd leave it until the next day. Until he'd had the chance to let it sink in a bit. Then he figured she would have to notice something was up with him and would ask what was wrong. But she didn't. She didn't ask what was wrong, so he waited longer. Days slipped by and turned into weeks and months. She should have known. She should have asked him. Eventually he decided to keep it to himself. She was too wrapped up in her own trivialities to be there for him when he needed her. She'd sit there making inane conversation and he'd stare straight at her without responding as she talked until her voice grew quiet and her story trailed off.

Hefin awoke to the stifled sounds of Dave and Rhian's lovemaking coming from the next room. He put his pillow over his head. Of course he was pleased for Dave. Dave was a nice guy and deserved a nice girl like Rhian. God knows Dave had been single long enough when Hefin himself had had lots of girlfriends. But he hated having to listen to them having sex. And there was no telling when he would hear it; it could be any time of day or night. It wasn't something he signed up for when he and Dave agreed to be housemates. But it wasn't exactly something you could hold against someone either, was it? It was an old building with shoddy partition walls. That was the problem. Other than that, it was the perfect house for them.

In a past incarnation the house had been a music shop. The kitchen was a pokey little room at the back, but the sitting room was an expansive space that took up almost the whole of downstairs and had big shop windows at the front. The lads were able to fit their rehearsal space into it alongside the sitting-room area without having to dismantle or move anything around. They called the space the Bandstand as that had been the name of the shop and was still painted over the front window outside.

He waited until a good ten or twenty minutes after the bed-creaks and breathy moans had reached their crescendo and subsided into silence before going into the bathroom for a shower and getting dressed. He went downstairs to the kitchen and got himself a bowl of cornflakes. He ate a few spoonfuls, then carried the bowl through to the Bandstand. He put it down on top of the piano and tinkered with the keys between mouthfuls. Soon he forgot about his breakfast as the music took over and he entered into playing 'Cantaloupe Island'.

'Hey, birthday boy!' said Rhian. He stopped playing and she gave him a hug. 'I'm going to get this place looking well lush for the party tonight.' Dave followed her into the room and slipped an arm around her waist. Hefin didn't hate them. No. He just wanted what they had.

Listening to music is a great source of enjoyment for many people. Nowadays you don't have to hear it live to appreciate it. Advances in recording and broadcasting means we can listen to wonderful music in the comfort of our homes.

Cari came home to the sight of Ben in his trackies and blue fleece dressing gown, sitting on the couch watching a DVD of a Frank Zappa documentary. 'Jesus, you're not even dressed,' she said. 'Were you smoking in the house?'

'Did you get anything for dinner?' he asked without looking at her.

'No.'

'Well, we'd better go into Porthcawl so. There's no food in the house.'

'What did you have for breakfast?'

'Just coffee. There's nothing there to eat.'

'And you couldn't go into town yourself to get anything?'

'I'm sick.'

'You're not sick. You're hungover. There is a difference.'

'Is there?'

'Yes, you're not supposed to get sympathy for a hangover.'

Ben stood up and yawned, stretching his arms up over his head, exposing his nascent paunch. With both hands, he scratched his thatch of salt and pepper hair. Cari turned away from him.

'I'll have a shower and then we can go,' he said.

Cari dropped her handbag on the floor. 'Oh for God's sake, Ben, I've had a full day at work. I'm tired and I'm starving. I don't want to go all the way into town to go shopping and then home again to cook.'

'Okay, so we'll eat out. And go straight to the Bandstand from there.'

'The Bandstand?'

'Oh yeah, Dave texted earlier. They're having a birthday party for Hefin.'

'Do we have to go to it?'

'Of course we do. They're in the band.'

126

'Fine, but I'm not drinking and we're coming home early.'

Cari thought about not going, about staying in and having a bath and getting a good night's sleep. But Ben would go anyway and stay out until all hours and she'd be awake wondering who was at the party and what was going on. She'd never been able to rest easy with him going out on his own. Eight years ago, she had been his other woman.

'You can't choose who you fall in love with,' he'd reassured her when guilty feelings got to her back then – back when she moved into the flat that he'd found for him and his fiancée, back when he was thirty-two and she was twenty. Now she was twenty-eight and he was forty.

B en sat in the middle of the couch, which had been pushed up against the wall to face the room. From there he could see everything that was happening at the party; a few people were dancing in the middle of the cleared floor of the Bandstand, others stood around chatting and munching on crisps and carrot sticks. Dave was at the computer doing his DJ thing. It may be 2005, Dave shouted to him, but a classic is a classic. He put on 'Birdland' and played air bass. At least he gauges the 'crowd reaction' as he calls it and mixes it up a bit, thought Ben. It was funny how the others acted like they discovered this music when he remembered it first time round. He enjoyed being young by proxy by hanging out with people ten or twenty years younger than him. Among musicians, it didn't matter what age you were – talent and a shared passion for music were all that counted. Forty sounds old. This here, my life, thought Ben, is not old.

He remembered a time when he thought getting older meant having your shit together. You were supposed to be married, own a house, have children, be into gardening and DIY. Somehow it just hadn't happened for him though. That was another reason he preferred to hang out with younger people. They didn't judge him the way people his own age did. He almost had a house once. He and his fiancée Amy had saved up enough between them for a deposit. But over the course of a few months of parties and gigs, the money had disappeared up his nose. After she discovered he'd blown their savings, Amy was all but done with him. Wales had been her idea. He'd never told her that his mother was from Wales. He'd never told anyone. The move was a last chance for them. A fresh start. Somewhere to live a quiet, wholesome life. Somewhere he could stay out of trouble. He'd gone on ahead to flat hunt. That's when he met Cari.

Hefin was letting loose on the dance floor with a handful of guests, when Cari and Ben let themselves in through the front door. He flinched in a moment of self-consciousness at Cari seeing him dance but he continued. Rhian had lined the whole place with candles. There was a table with finger food and now-empty cocktail jugs. So much better than the slapdash piss-ups he and Dave had hosted in the past. Benny Goodman's 'Sing, Sing, Sing' pounded from the amps hooked up to Dave's Mac. Hefin's upright piano was in the same place as always, facing the rehearsal space, and the drums and other equipment had been moved to the sides leaving a clear area to serve as a dance floor. Ben gave Hefin a slap on the back, said 'Happy birthday, old man!' and handed him a bottle of gin.

'Thanks. I'm old, but I'm not that old yet.' He winked.

'Yeah, enjoy it while you can. Just another ten years before you get to my age and start getting the grey hair and wrinkles!' Ben laughed.

128

Hefin danced his way over to Cari. She wished him a happy birthday and as she leaned forward to give him a kiss on the cheek, he turned his head so it landed on his lips. She looked surprised; he looked innocently back at her and resumed dancing. Ben opened a bottle of beer and handed it to Cari. She took a lengthy swig.

'C'mon, dance, you two. It's my birthday!' said Hefin, waving his arms, bouncing from foot to foot. Ben laughed a 'fat chance' laugh and went to do the rounds of greeting everyone at the party.

Hefin didn't normally let on when he was drunk, but he'd had a few cocktails and was giving himself over to celebrating his birthday. 'C'mon, Cari!' He put his hands on her waist. Her waist felt like he'd expected it to feel. She took another swig of her beer and laughed. 'Let me have one more of these – then I'll dance,' she said.

You can make a simple musical instrument by blowing across the mouth of a medicine bottle. Experiment with making different notes by varying the amount of liquid in the bottle.

Cari felt the smooth glass between her lips, the cold familiar tang promising to banish her tiredness. She joined Rhian and the other girls chatting by the food table and finished her beer quickly. In the kitchen she opened her large handbag and took out the bottle of vodka she'd brought with her just in case. Better looking at it than looking for it, her mother used to say, though admittedly not about bottles of vodka. Cari hadn't planned to drink but this wasn't really drinking – this was a strategic move to stay awake. She made a fist around the lid and twisted; it clicked as the perforated seal broke. Thin metal sang against glass as she unscrewed the lid. She poured vodka into a mug and added tonic, blew across the top of the bottle to make a musical note. It was a habit she'd had since childhood. Since her mother used to teach her about music when she was old enough to learn but too young to go to school. She replaced the lid, then hid the bottle in her bag again. Not that she didn't want to share it; it's just that at this kind of party the whole lot might disappear in minutes if she left it out on the table.

B en could see, from his place on the couch, into the kitchen and through the back window to where Cari was out on the decking with Hefin. Every now and then someone coming in or out of the kitchen broke his view of them, but he could make out that they were leaning on the railings and smoking. Sometimes, when he saw her from afar like this, he wondered if he would fall in love with her if he met her now. Would her body, a layer thicker now all over, appeal to him? Her dyed black hair that only came to just below her ears. He thought if she were a stranger, he'd find her sexy, just in a different way to when he first met her. Back then it was her naivety that attracted him. He had watched her through the window of a hotel function room. He had been out in the dark and cold, and there she was in the bright warmth, her slender fingers plucking gracefully at the strings of a harp. Her hair was long then, mousey brown and so soft. He'd gatecrashed the wedding. He had to. He had to hear her play, had to talk to her. When she stood up, he saw her tall, lithe figure was draped in a peach silk dress that made clear the contours of her shoulders, breasts, hips.

In the years since they'd been together, she had developed a worldly look of experience about her, a glint of boldness in her eye. Out on the decking now she looked solid in her tight black dress. She was wearing a fedora hat, black eye make-up and red lipstick. She had become the jazz chic on his arm. He watched through the window as she flicked her head back laughing at something Hefin said. She leaned in again. They seemed to move a few inches towards each other, close the gap between the sides of their bodies.

A girl in a black beret sat next to him and said, 'Hey, I saw you guys play last night. You were amazing!'

'Thanks.'

'Seriously amazing gig.'

'Thanks.'

She wasn't going away. Hefin and Cari were still outside.

'I play a bit myself, you know,' said the girl with the beret.

'Really?'

'Yeah. I write songs all the time. I'll play one for you . . .' She picked up a guitar – the old one Dave left lying around so no one would touch his – and started strumming and clearing her throat, and strumming and stopping and saying, 'Oh that wasn't right, I'll start again.' Ben could barely hear her, but she was singing an okay song so he tried to pay her some attention. Beginners could do with encouragement from established musicians like him. Cari came back into the party with Rhian and raised her eyebrows at him.

She went over to the girls and whatever they were saying was completely inaudible to him over the music coming from the speakers and the girl singing in his ear. Then they were all dancing, Cari and the other girls, though none of them were girls really any more.

Hefin's cigarette smoke wafted into the kitchen through the open back door from the decking where he stood by himself. Cari followed the smoke. She leaned down to the pouch of Amber Leaf Hefin held in his hand and put her ear to it.

'Yes?' she said.

'What are you doing?' asked Hefin laughing.

'Your tobacco was calling me. I heard it from inside.'

'I thought you'd given up.'

'Well, I had but . . .'

'Ah yes, wait you're right . . . I hear it now.' He held the pouch up to his ear. 'It says it's okay for you to smoke because it's my birthday.'

He handed it to her. She pulled a cigarette's worth from the wad, tearing it like moss from a tree. She arranged it along the crease of the flimsy paper and rolled it between her thumbs, index and middle fingers. Hefin watched intently as she raised the cigarette to her mouth and licked the seal shut.

'Nicely done,' he said, taking a drag from his own rollie.

'Thank you,' said Cari. She held it up in admiration for a moment before placing it between her lips and lighting it from the flame Hefin proffered. The excess paper flared for a moment, then subsided into a glow.

'You having a good birthday?'

'Yes, thank you. Thanks for coming out on a weeknight.'

'My pleasure.'

They leaned on the railings, looking out at the overgrown garden. In the moonlight Hefin felt like they were black and white, like in some old movie where men light women's cigarettes for them.

'I don't know how you do it,' said Hefin. 'Going out so much and then getting up for work in the mornings.'

'Ah, I'm used to it. I just get a really good sleep at weekends.'

'But you work all day and then . . . you do all the cooking, don't you?'

'I like cooking.'

'Does Ben ever have a meal waiting for you when you come in?'

'Actually, we went out for dinner this evening. And he paid.'

'But you pay the rent, don't you? Sorry, I'm drunk. It's none of my business.' He wasn't sorry. For a long time he'd wanted to point out all of the ways in which Ben was an incompetent boyfriend.

'No, no, it's okay. That's the arrangement we've always had. I have a regular income so I pay the rent, and he pays for all our drinks when we're out.'

'I didn't mean to pry. I just . . . well, you're lovely and I just hope he doesn't take you for granted.'

Cari gave a lopsided smile and took a drag, looking out at the weeds. Hefin moved a little closer to her.

'You know there's more to him than you think,' said Cari. 'He's had his troubles too.'

'Really? I find that hard to believe. He's always so—'

'You know his mother disappeared when he was young?'

'I thought his parents split up.'

'That's what he lets people believe.'

'So, she abandoned him and his dad?'

Cari shrugged. 'I don't know. He said she left all her stuff behind. They reported her as a missing person. He was seven. Can you imagine? Seven?' She thought about telling him how Ben had looked for his mother for years when he was a child, how he'd cycled around after school every day, searching for clues. That he'd spent his pocket money on photocopies of a poster he had made, with her picture and the words 'Have you seen Tegan Deane?' but to tell Hefin all that felt like it would be a betrayal.

'But how come he never—'

Rhian appeared in the doorway.

'Cari, you've got to come dance!' Cari threw the glowing butt of her cigarette into the wet grass beyond the decking and allowed herself to be dragged back into the party, which was by now filling up with people.

Hefin was left standing alone outside in the dark. He watched Cari through the window as she moved her hips to the music playing inside. Then he spotted Ben, sitting on the couch, looking straight at him. Or else at his own reflection, Hefin couldn't tell. He coolly finished his rollie and went back inside.

Young people like to gather in each other's houses and listen to records together. In this way they share and discover new music.

Cari placed the empty vodka bottle on the kitchen table and picked up wine bottle after wine bottle until she found one with something in it. She poured it into her mug and went back to the sitting room. She stood at the edge of the dance area. Ben was still on the couch, head cocked to one side watching a girl in a beret strum on a guitar. Cari recognised her face from around town. She was about twenty and had long brown hair and was incredibly thin.

'Who's the new girl?' Cari asked Rhian, nodding her head in the direction of the guitar recital without looking that way.

'I don't know. But someone should buy her a burger.'

Cari laughed and danced, red wine blurring everything to soft focus. Her boots were beginning to hurt so, still dancing, she unzipped one and tried to pull it off. Rhian grabbed her from behind under the arms and two of the other girls grabbed the boot and pulled it off. Laughing, they took off the other one the same way and flung it across the room where it landed at Hefin's feet. He picked it up and sniffed it, then threw his head back and rolled his eyes in mock ecstasy. Steely Dan were singing 'My Old School' and Hefin bounded over to Cari and led her in a dance, pulling her to him and pushing her away, twirling her around, his hands going from holding hers to her waist and back again.

As the night went on people drifted off home and soon there was just the band and a handful of others left. Beret-girl was keeled over asleep on the couch taking up the two spaces next to Ben. Every now and then she opened her eyes and half sat up pretending to be awake and then drifted off again. The room was in almost complete darkness; most of the candles had burned out and there was just one lamp on. The no smoking in the house rule had been forgotten and a joint was passed around. Dave had given up DJing. He sat on the floor, picked up a guitar and sang 'The Girl from Ipanema'. Everyone who was still conscious tried to sing along. Then he gave the guitar to Ben, who muttered something about being a drummer and not really able to play guitar and then silenced everyone with 'Hallelujah'. His floppy dark hair had always been one of the things Cari had liked about him, that ruffled, effortless mop, but as it became more and more grey, it gave him a coarse, dishevelled look, more down-and-out than just-out-of-bed and his stubble was grey now, too. Her attitude softened as she watched and listened to him play. She remembered how much she loved him. All that other stuff, she thought – work and daytime and bills – meant nothing. None of that was real. This was what mattered: friends and good times and living and loving while you're alive.

135

Hefin stood up and sat at the piano. 'I'm not sure I have all the words to this yet,' he said. 'But it's my birthday and I'm too drunk to care. And anyway, it's my own song so no one will know if I make any mistakes.' His fingers danced slowly on the keys and he sang lyrics about holding out for someone to love. It was a slow, soulful song. Cari's breath caught in her chest and she felt like she needed to get out of there but at the same time wanted to stay in that moment for ever, letting the song run through her. Hefin looked so good, his skin glowing by candlelight, his eyes sparking when he opened them. Unlike most of the other musicians he kept his dark-blond hair neat and short. She'd always known he was good-looking but she'd never thought of him as attractive before tonight. Not to her. She stared at the floor. She needed to shake those thoughts from her mind. It was just the drink.

Ben's eyes were focused on one large candle that was still burning in the centre of the cluttered coffee table. Dave took up the guitar and played 'The Girl from Ipanema'. It was a song Ben's mother used to put on the record player when he was little. She'd dance around the house with him and call him the handsomest man in all of England. That was one of his memories. 'Do you remember her?' That is what people always asked when he told them about her going missing. Not that he told many people. Only when he got to know them and only if he liked them. For others he remained vague on the whole issue; saying his mother lived in London sufficed to stop people's questions. Usually when people asked him if he remembered her, he'd answer, 'Yeah, a bit.' Cari was the only person he'd ever really explained it to. It was like he had an archive of memories, he'd told her, like short home movies filmed from his point of view. He could see them all perfectly, just a minute or two of memory time for each. Staring at the candle flame, he tried to recall them all now. Cycling along the river path with his dad and her was one of them. Her smiling and waving goodbye to him on his first day of school was another. On a sunny day, her pointing out a white flower and teaching him that it was called stitchwort.

A ripple of applause broke his reverie. Dave held the guitar out to Ben.

'I can't follow that. I'm a drummer,' said Ben.

'Ah, just one song.'

'I only know about three chords.'

'That's all you need,' said Dave.

There was a communal murmur egging him on until he took the guitar. He sang 'Hallelujah'. He knew he did a good job. After a stunned silence, everyone clapped and he held out the guitar and said, 'Who's next?'

Hefin sat down at the piano and sang something he'd written himself. It was good. Ben hadn't heard it before. He wondered how many other songs Hefin had written that he hadn't shared with the band. While Hefin sang and all eyes were on him, or closed, Ben looked around. Less than ten people in the room. The diehards, succumbing to gravity and tiredness, sprawled in armchairs and on cushions on the floor. Rhian lay on the floor resting her head on Dave's lap. Cari was on the floor leaning against an armchair, looking hypnotised by Hefin's song.

His mother was younger than Cari was now when she disappeared. And he was older than his father was when it happened. It was strange, he thought, a thing that really bothered him when his father told him she'd been found, was that after all this time, after all his imaginings about where she had gone and why, the idea of her having an affair had never entered his mind.

Hefin gave Cari a hug goodbye at the door and as he did, with one hand behind her shoulder blades and one on her lower back, he pressed the length of her body against his. He gave Ben a quick man hug. It had irked him increasingly lately to see Cari leave with Ben. He felt displaced, though he knew there was no logic to the feeling. Ben and Cari had been together since long before he'd known them.

He walked back through the devastation of beer cans and glasses and assorted candleholders and cups used as ashtrays and bits of mushed cake on paper plates. Dave and Rhian had already gone up to bed. That girl in the beret, now not-so-fashionably askew, was asleep on the couch. He thought about waking her to see if she needed a taxi. He thought about waking her to see if he could score with her. He decided both ideas were too much bother, got himself a pint of water and some paracetamol and went upstairs.

In bed, he picked up his phone and thought for a moment. He wrote a text – a casual one to send to both Ben and Cari's phones: 'Thanks guys for coming to my party. Was a great night!' Four minutes later a beep . . . from Cari. 'It was a pleasure. Glad you enjoyed your birthday.'

Though the triangle looks like a simple instrument, it is in fact difficult to play well.

Cari woke the next morning, or rather a few hours later, with remnants of dreams in her head – this time about Hefin. She couldn't remember the words of his song, but she could feel it under her skin. It dried and cracked. Work was another painful treadmill of a day. Never again, she told herself, passing the off-licence on her way home. When she got in, Ben was on the couch watching *The Simpsons*. 'I'm sick,' he said. She ignored him and unpacked some groceries from her handbag. She put pasta on to boil and opened a jar of pesto.

After dinner in front of the TV, she left the dishes on the coffee table, her eyes hot with tiredness, and stood up.

'Goodnight,' she said.

'What? But it's only eight o'clock.'

'I'm shattered.'

'What am I supposed to do now? I won't be able to sleep for hours. Did you get any booze?'

'No. Goodnight.'

Ben leaned up for a kiss and Cari turned away.

'You stink of fags.'

'I saw you smoking at the party.'

She trudged through the hallway to the bedroom, stripped to her underwear and got straight into bed without brushing her teeth. She lay there fitfully turning, wishing for sleep. She was hot and cold, and visions came to her from the night before. Every time she was about to drop off her body gave a twitch and woke her up again. She started to think about her school friends and how many of them were married and owned houses and had children and proper careers. She put her own life in one side of the scales and theirs in the other and it tipped so hard she thought she might catapult herself out of the life she was in with those thoughts.

Next day she was relieved to feel close to normal again. She got through work and when Ben got ready to go to his gig in the evening, she decided to stay in. She didn't even decide – it was simply the only thing she could do; her body would not let her go out again. She was too tired to care about who would be at the gig and what she would miss. She went to bed as soon as Ben left the flat and was asleep before people would even be arriving at the bar he was playing in.

She was woken by the sound of Ben stumbling around the room, taking off his jeans. The room filled with a smell of beer. It was dark. She reached out her hand and picked up her phone on the bedside table. Her alarm was set to go off in fifteen minutes. Ben fell into the bed, lobbed one arm across her.

'Hey, Sugartits,' he slurred.

She turned her head away from him and covered her mouth with duvet to take a breath. He threw a heavy leg across her. She wriggled out from under him and stood up.

'Oh, Hefin's staying on the couch,' Ben mumbled. 'He came back for a drink after the gig.'

Ben was snoring by the time Cari got out of the shower. She looked at him closely, the way you only get the chance to when someone is asleep. He seemed so vulnerable and innocent, like a sleeping child. Seeing him like that reminded her that he was once someone's baby, worthy of love and protection, and then she felt ashamed for being disgusted by him. She wondered about his ex he'd left to be with her and the life in London he'd left behind. What was it like at the end for them? Had he been so shut off from her as well? She'd begun to wonder more and more lately what went on inside his head.

She got dressed and tiptoed down the corridor into the curtain-dark sitting room. Hefin was lying on the couch, under a duvet, watching a film. His shoes and jeans were in a heap on the floor. He swivelled round and sat up when she came down.

'Morning,' he smiled at her. 'You look how I'd like to feel.'

'What?'

'I mean you look so fresh . . . and healthy . . . and beautiful. How do you do that at . . .' He looked at his phone. '7.21 a.m.?'

'Thank you. Ignore me. I'll be gone in a while. I'm just grabbing some breakfast.'

'Ah, I can't sleep anyway.'

'Well do you want a cup of tea then?'

'That, Cari my darling, would be wonderful.'

She went into the kitchen and reappeared with a mug for him.

'Where's yours? Aren't you going to join me?'

'Well . . . okay.' She brought her own mug and a plate of toast through and sat on the couch beside him. He was watching *Casablanca*.

'I forgot we even had this DVD,' she said. 'I love this film.'

'Me too.'

Cari sipped her tea and began quoting a line from the film.

Hefin joined in and looking at each other they finished the quote in unison.

'Call in sick,' said Hefin.

'What? I can't do that.'

'Of course you can. Call in sick.'

'No.'

'What would you really rather do today, go to a job you hate in an office with old grannies or stay here with me watching movies?' He threw the duvet over her lap to cover them both and picked up an almost full bottle of wine from the floor. He swigged from it, then held it out to her. 'Come on, Cari, be decadent.'

Ben dreamed he was outside a locked toilet door trying to get in. He came to consciousness and realised he was bursting to go. Cari's side of the bed was empty. She must have already gone to work. He was still quite drunk and bed was so comfortable he really didn't want to get out of it, so he lay there for a while trying to ignore the urge in the hope that it would go away and he'd fall asleep again. Eventually he got up and went to the bathroom. He could hear the sound of 'As Time Goes By' coming from the living room. Hefin must be listening to it, he thought. He pissed and went back to bed.

He was grateful for the sound of the song. He couldn't stand silence. When he wasn't drunk he needed to listen to music or the radio to go to sleep. Silence reminded him of the atmosphere in his father's house when he was growing up and the absence of sound that was left by his mother's going away. It was at once a feeling of emptiness and of dread. It was a feeling that something was missing and something awful was readying itself to rush into the space, like warm air being pushed out by a cold draught.

Back then, he played records to fill the void, to cover the maddening, quiet rasp of his father slowly turning the pages of his stamp albums, lest the sound of it drive him to beat him over the head with them the way he fantasised about doing. Why hadn't his father been out there doing something? Why hadn't he looked for her properly instead of sitting there passively waiting for her to come back? Waiting for the police to do their job. Before the song was over Ben was asleep.

When he came to the hangover was setting in. He went to the bathroom where he washed down some Neurofen with a glass of water. The sitting room was silent. Hefin must be asleep or gone home, he thought. As he climbed back into bed he put his head to Cari's pillow and smelled her perfume. He wished she didn't have to go to work every day and leave him alone. He put on the radio and drifted off to sleep again.

Hefin handed Cari the bottle. She blew across the top of it and it made a pleasant resonant sound. She took a swig.

'I'd better make that call,' she said and stood up. She handed the bottle back to Hefin, who was smiling with approval. When she went to the kitchen and he could hear her murmuring her excuses, he paused the film and went to the bathroom. He pissed, splashed his face with cold water and checked himself in the mirror. He took a deep breath and went back to the couch just as she came back to it, too. They both sat down. He felt like an agreement had passed between them with that swig of wine she'd taken. They had entered into something.

'I can't believe I just did that. I never call in sick,' she said. 'You're a bad influence on me.'

'I didn't make you do anything.' Hefin smiled innocently as if mitching work had been her idea. 'You're your own person.'

She pulled her legs up onto the couch and crossed them; her right knee rested against his thigh. He buzzed with the clandestine intimacy. He replaced the duvet across their legs. She picked up the bottle, took another swig and giggled. Then she blew into the throat of the bottle and it gave out a note again.

'Very musical,' said Hefin. 'Did you ever play an instrument, Cari?'

'Yeah. I played the harp. Mind you, it's been so long since I've played I think I've forgotten how to.' She passed him the bottle. 'I started when I was seven and kept going with it for years. I used to make a nice bit of pocket money playing for weddings.'

'You know Ben never even mentioned that you play the harp.' Actually, he might have; the information did ring a bell with Hefin but he couldn't remember an exact time Ben had mentioned it.

'Well, the harp doesn't exactly fit in with the jazz scene, does it? And it literally didn't fit into this flat, so I left it at my parents' house.'

'I can't imagine ever giving up playing.' Hefin shook his head. 'Cari, that is a tragedy. You should never compromise who you are for anything or anyone.'

'But I must not have loved it that much if I left it behind though, right? That's what Ben says anyway.'

Hefin passed her the bottle. She drank. She blew. The notes coming from the bottle were getting lower in tone. When she passed the bottle back to Hefin he wrapped his hand around it in such a way that his fingers briefly overlapped with hers.

'So, you play the harp, eh?' said Hefin, bemused.

'Played.'

'There's so much I don't know about you, Cari.'

'There's a lot I don't know about you, Hefin.'

'Well, I've got all day.'

'Apparently I have now, too.'

The bottle went back and forth between them and they became more relaxed as they recounted stories. They swapped tales of teenage drinking escapades, of the best concerts they'd ever been to, trouble they'd got into at school, they discussed who they would want to meet if they could meet anyone in history, places they had travelled to and would like to go. He told her about his friends in Port Talbot. She asked him how he got into music and he told her about his mother who played clarinet in the National Orchestra of Wales and how he was raised on classical music. He told her music was intrinsic to his being and at 8 a.m., over a bottle of wine, it didn't seem at all melodramatic to say that. It was fitting. It seemed a good time to bare his soul. Cari's parents both played music when she was growing up, too, she said. Folk music. She understood about it being in the blood.

'They're still together, and I think they're happy,' Cari replied when Hefin asked about her parents.

'Mine, too. Maybe that's why I'm so dysfunctional,' said Hefin.

'Yeah, coming from a stable home is a disadvantage these days, isn't it? No one understands how deprived we are. I mean other people have divorced parents and dead parents and alcoholics and poverty and all sorts to blame for their fucked-up states of being. We got nothing,' said Cari. She was facing him completely.

'We've got a lot in common, you and me, Cari, haven't we?' Hefin held eye contact with her. They sat locked in that look for a long moment. Then – in a split second – Hefin was suddenly highly aware that this was his bandmate's girlfriend and this was a big deal, not some random girl at a party and he took a breath, turned to the paused image on the TV screen and said, 'Hey, are we going to watch this film or what?'

Cari held up the wine bottle and let the last few drops drip into her mouth from above.

'Sure.'

He hit play and they both sat back on the sofa, side by side. Black and white Bogart took over their attention. Or at least Hefin pretended he did. He was reeling inside at the proximity of Cari's body to his. They both slid down a bit to get more comfortable, pulling the duvet up over their stomachs. Now their sides were in contact shoulder to knee. After a few minutes Cari snuggled her head casually sideways into Hefin's shoulder. This is fine, thought Hefin. Friends watch films together. Cari pulled her legs up to the side and lay with her head on Hefin's lap, keeping her head facing the screen, moving with a slowness that could be interpreted as sleepiness, as if her movements were done in a sort of unconscious state, the way one might accidentally lean on a stranger on an aeroplane. This is fine, thought Hefin. Friends do this. Then he put his hand tentatively near her head so it lay on some of her hair. This is fine, thought Hefin. Ben doesn't deserve her. On screen a man began playing piano in a gin bar. Hefin's fingers stirred with the notes, in micro-movements at first then in small strokes across Cari's hair, from her temple back across her head, slowly, over and again. *A kiss is just a kiss*, sang the man on the screen. Cari's head turned and she looked up at Hefin. He leaned forward.

An experienced and charismatic conductor can completely transform the sound of an orchestra. He seems to have mysterious powers as he communicates what he wants, not just with waving gestures, but at times with the tiniest of motions of his fingers or eyes, resulting in the most splendid music.

Cari stood in front of the mirror in the bedroom, adding the finishing touches to her outfit. She smiled as she tied a belt on a pair of trousers that had been too tight for her two months before. In fact, she remembered that she'd been unable to put them on for work the morning of *Casablanca* because she couldn't close them. She put on lipstick and

146

puckered her lips. She knew she was looking good. She was feeling more and more like her old self and at the same time she felt brand new, like she could tear off a skin she'd been contained in for too long.

She was spritzing herself with perfume when Ben walked in and put his arms around her. She put the bottle on the chest of drawers, unwrapped his arms from her waist and pushed them away. Ben sniffed.

'Is that a new perfume?'

'Oh yeah. I got it the other day in Cardiff.'

'But it's your birthday next week. You could have told me you needed some and I'd have got it for you.'

'Yeah, sorry, I just thought I'd pick one up while I was there.'

Ben looked at the bottle, shaped like a woman's torso, filled with pink fragrance.

'It's different to the one I get you.'

'Yeah, I just fancied a change. Do you not like it? You can still get me a bottle of the other one if you want.'

'No, I'll have to get you something else now.'

Cari took the bottle off the chest of drawers and stuffed it into a bag of toiletries. Ben sat on the bed watching her as she chose a necklace by holding various ones up to her neck.

'Why are you looking at me like that?' said Cari.

'Like what? Am I not allowed to look at you now?'

'Don't be silly.' Cari put two different shoes on and alternated standing on one leg to see which one looked better with her outfit.

'It's been really nice that you've been coming to so many gigs lately. It's like old times, having you there, right up the front.'

'Yeah.'

'I do notice, you know. It makes a difference to me, to my performance, seeing you there enjoying the music.'

'Yeah, great.'

'You look hot.'

'Thanks,' she said without looking at him. His compliments were never really compliments. He would tell her she *looked* 'really nice' or that a dress looked good on her. He never told her that *she* herself was beautiful or pretty. He was never mesmerised by her eyes or her smile the way Hefin was or told her she was utterly gorgeous like Hefin had told her the day he gave her the present of perfume in Cardiff. They had met there for a day to really spend time together, not just grabbing kisses when Ben was out of the room. They'd gone shopping in a department store the way any couple would. They had held hands under the table when they went for brunch. And, pretending they hadn't both planned it in their heads, pretending it was a spontaneous idea, an urge they had no control over, an unpremeditated thing, they rented a hotel room.

'Why do we have to go all the way to Port Talbot for a party anyway?' Ben asked, checking his tousled hair in the mirror.

'You said yourself, Hefin's always wanted us to meet his friends. And it's nice to say yes when someone gives you an invitation.'

'I know, but I don't know if I can be bothered now. I mean he's in the band and all but he's not really that close a friend, is he?'

'The taxi's on its way to pick us up.'

Ben was in a better mood by the time they got to the party. Cari was right, he thought, it was good to get out and do something different. The place was heaving with people and it

148

was a proper big party. There seemed to be people aged seventeen to seventy there. There was a bong on the kitchen table with an old guy with long grey hair and a beard at the helm. The sitting room had disco lights going, covering dancing faces with different-coloured dots. The crowd spilled out of the back door onto the patio. Hefin introduced them to one person after another. Within half an hour they had a multitude of new best friends.

It was the first time Ben had been to a good party since London. It reminded him of the ones he used to wind up at every night that first summer, after he'd done his A levels, when he'd worked in a bar in Camden and lived in a room over it. He'd had such a good time that summer he'd almost forgotten his secret hunch that his mother had gone to London and his fantasy of bumping into her there someday.

They stood in the kitchen, chatting to various people coming in and out. Ben having been introduced as Hefin's bandmate, one girl asked him what instrument he played. She was very beautiful in a natural sort of way; she had a wavy mane of blonde hair, soft features and a silver nose ring.

'What made you choose the drums?' she asked. He thought about it. Sometimes it was easier to be honest with complete strangers than with people he knew.

'You know what? I think I just needed to hit something.'

He expected the girl to laugh but instead she nodded understandingly.

'Yeah, I get that,' she said.

'My mother left when I was a kid and . . .'

'I'm sorry to hear that,' said the girl.

Cari was looking around, not listening to the conversation.

'Thanks, it's okay. It's just, well, the house was so quiet after she left that I suppose on some level I wanted to fill it with sound, with music. Does that sound stupid?'

'Not at all,' said the girl. 'You know I read somewhere that playing music is a way of reintegrating the self with the universal self.'

'That's deep.'

'Isn't it?' The girl smiled. Then she caught Cari's attention. 'Do you play an instrument, Cari, isn't it?'

'No,' said Cari so brusquely that the girl soon wandered off.

'Jesus, Cari,' Ben said. 'That was a bit rude.'

'No, it wasn't. She asked me a question and I answered it. Anyway, speaking of rude, Hefin's kind of abandoned us, hasn't he?'

'What?'

'Well, I mean he invited us here and he's barely spoken to us since we arrived.'

'He just introduced us to all of his friends. Isn't that why you made us come here in the first place, to meet his friends? And be polite?'

Cari didn't answer.

'There are lots of cool people here,' said Ben. 'I'm having a good time.' He turned to the old guy who was offering him a hit of the bong and said no thanks. He wasn't sure if it was that drugs were no good any more or if they affected him differently now from the way they did years ago, but he was happy enough with a few beers.

'C'mon, let's check out the garden,' he suggested. He and Cari went through the back door to where a bonfire was blazing and people sat around it on kitchen chairs and on benches made from pallets. Ben and Cari sat down on a pallet with everyone nodding hellos to them as they did so. A set of bongos was sitting idle on the opposite side of the fire. Ben thought about what the blonde girl had said about reintegrating the self through playing music. It seemed very wise and true. He couldn't resist. He asked someone to pass the bongos to him. He wedged them between his legs and began tapping out a rhythm. Everyone looked at Ben and some of them began nodding their heads and tapping their feet in time. Cari refilled her mug with vodka from her bag, exposing only the bottle neck. 'I'm going to find a mixer,' she said and went back into the house. A couple of minutes later a guy sat down in her spot, smiled at Ben and said, 'Nice playing.'

Ben lost track of time as he drummed and when he drank the last bit of his beer it was warm. He handed the bongos to the bloke who'd been sitting next to him and went inside to get another drink.

In the kitchen Cari was standing with her back to the room, not talking to anyone. She was half next to, half in the doorway to the sitting room, staring intently at something Ben couldn't see. Her face was flushed red and her lips pursed in anger. She gulped at her mug the way someone readying themselves to do something drains the last of a mug of tea.

The old man at the kitchen table proffered Ben the empty chair next to him. 'Sit, sit,' he said.

Ben waved a polite refusal. Cari was so absorbed in what she was staring at that she didn't notice Ben was in the room.

'You know we've only got seven years left before the Mayan calendar runs out,' said the old man. Ben pretended he hadn't heard him.

Cari poured the end of her vodka into her mug and knocked it back neat. Ben stood right behind her and saw what she was staring at: Hefin locked in a kiss with the blonde girl with the nose ring. Cari put the empty bottle and the mug down on the counter and staggered forward into the sitting room.

Hefin felt like he'd been kicked hard in the gut when he saw Cari arrive at the party with Ben. He had only invited her. He'd convinced himself that she had broken up with Ben and would be there on her own, single, and they could be together at last. He had fantasised about introducing her to all his friends. Now he was having to introduce Ben and Cari to them instead. He began to wish he'd never met either of them. How could Cari not understand how it felt for him to see the woman he was in love with, the woman he was supposed to be with, with someone else?

He had explained it to her the week before when they met in Cardiff. They'd spent the best part of that day in a hotel room where they had finally been able to be free with each other. Their lovemaking – for that was what it was for Hefin at least – was urgent, by turns slow and unrestrained. Afterwards they'd luxuriated in lying naked together, seeing and caressing each other's bodies. When they'd recovered enough they did it again. And again. They made up for the hurried trysts while Dave was out of the house at the Bandstand and the careful, silent sex in the early hours while Ben slept. That day in the hotel room, overcome with a feeling of belonging, Hefin had told her he loved her, and she had reciprocated. He told her he couldn't stand to see her with Ben any more. She had promised to break up with Ben.

How could she be so spineless and cold as to turn up here with him and parade around like everything was fine? He would make sure she knew how it felt to see the person you love with someone else. And if she did really love him, she'd leave Ben. He started talking to a blonde girl with a nose ring, a girl he knew fancied him. He turned on his charm. He flirted with her, while Cari stood in the doorway watching them. Every now and then he'd look up to make sure Cari could see him touch the girl's hair or see the girl laugh at something he said. He made expressionless eye contact with Cari. Then he kissed the girl. He kissed her slowly and passionately; he closed his eyes. He could feel Cari watching. He didn't even know if he was in love with her or if he hated her in that moment. He just knew he needed her to know how it felt.

He kissed the girl for a long time at the side of the loud and crowded room. When he opened his eyes Cari was just a few feet away from him, right in his sightline, wavering in drunkenness behind the girl. She was whispering something to a guy with dreadlocks. The guy responded with a grin and they kissed. The blonde girl was saying something to Hefin but it wasn't going in. He spotted Ben in the doorway, where Cari had been standing. Ben's face was contorted with disbelief as Cari kissed the dreadlocked guy. For a split-second Ben looked at Hefin as if searching for an answer, then he crossed to the middle of the room, through people bumping into him as they danced, to Cari and the guy.

Ben put his hands on their shoulders and pushed them apart. The guy was easy to shove aside; he wasn't the aggressive type, he just looked puzzled. Ben looked at Cari with intensity, searching her face.

'Cari, what are you doing?'

Cari looked stunned. 'I . . .'

'You're breaking my heart.'

The dreadlocked guy took a step backwards.

'It's not . . . I didn't mean . . .' stuttered Cari.

'My mother was murdered,' Ben blurted out at her.

'Woah,' said the dreadlocked guy.

'Oh my God, Ben.' She put her arms out to him and her face turned to absolute concern as if for an injured child. As she went to hug him he moved back. Then she turned her head and looked at him sideways. 'When did you find out? How long have you known?'

'I wanted to tell you.' His eyes welled up. He stepped towards her. She took his hands.

The dreadlocked guy and the few people who had noticed the kissing incident turned back to dancing and conversation. Hefin, unwatched by anyone, slipped out the front door. When he got far enough away from the house he crouched in the darkness and let the tears come. He wondered if Ben had figured out what had been happening in that room. Then he realised that even if he had, it would probably never matter and never be spoken about.

We are all born with a musical instrument, though many of us forget to think of it as one – it is of course our voice.

Flight Adventure India

*India may strike you as a country of contrasts. It is rich with
colour and beauty in its landscapes, buildings, traditions and
people, and at the same time there is great poverty. Some places
are very noisy and hectic and others are wonderfully peaceful.
For anyone who travels there it certainly is an experience they
will never forget.*

Looking out of the plane window over miles and miles of
red mountainous desert landscape into a blue-yellow-
pink-purple sunset many thoughts whispered through Kristi's
mind, but one kept rising loudly to the surface: 'I'm doing it.
I'm really doing it.'

She'd left Ireland with all its godforsaken mildew and pre-
cipitation behind and was on an adventure. A real one – not
just a road trip to Bundoran or Lahinch. She didn't even care
what Fergus might be up to – likelihood was he was in the local
pub having the same conversations with the same locals he did
every weekend anyway. They'd be sitting around talking about

all the great plans and intentions they would never carry out. Drink-talk Fergus had called it, explaining to her, when she was still fairly new in Ireland, that it was perfectly understood that if you arranged to do something with someone over a few pints, neither party ever really expected it to happen.

It was still dark when the plane arrived in Mumbai at 5 a.m. Getting off the plane the warmth of the air felt familiar to her, like it did back home in California, but it was thick with a mélange of unfamiliar odours, at once fetid and fragrant. How long since her senses had experienced something completely new? All the things she'd read in guidebooks and heard from others about the poverty came to her mind as she looked around the arrivals' hall. It looked like a disused, dilapidated school hall with a dirty, cracked linoleum floor.

By the time she retrieved her rucksack from the carousel lazily turning bags on a crooked U amidst shouting, shoving Indians she felt panicky. There was no way back. She couldn't just get back on the plane and go home. She couldn't just go home to Fergus. No. This was the whole point of it – to be independent. To be strong. To be the woman she could not be around him and to do things that he would never do with her.

She hoped there would be taxis at this hour. Then the doors opened to the outside as the first passengers left the building. Shouts from touts and heated haggling formed the sound of chaos. A throng of Indian men and boys swelled against a barrier shouting 'taxi taxi taxi!'

When she stepped outside they went crazy like fish at feeding time at the surface of a tank, shoving one another aside, encircling her. Cars from earlier decades lined up. 'Rickshaw rickshaw rickshaw!' 'Madam taxi, taxi madam!' They tried to steer her into their vehicles by way of showing her with a flourish of the hand just how ready theirs was, their hand doubling as a weapon with which to bat other drivers aside. She froze. They grew more frantic. An Indian girl giggled and hid her eyes from Kristi.

She tried to catch the eyes of any of the Europeans from the flight so that she could form an express friendship and share a taxi. She watched a group of Scandinavians, who appeared to be bickering amongst themselves, get into two taxis and leave. Car by car she watched the arrivals area empty of Westerners until there was just one couple left. They looked friendly. No, they replied, they weren't going to the centre. They were flying straight on to Goa.

Once she was inside a taxi the other drivers backed off, having lost the battle for her custom. She held up a piece of paper for the driver that had on it the address of a hotel recommended by the *Lonely Planet* guidebook. He glanced in the direction of the page and waved his hand. 'Hotel. Yes? Hotel,' and took off, motor buzzing, weaving in and out, beeping at the rest of the beeping taxis. There appeared to be no set sides of the road nor lanes, just a river of traffic.

'What country?' asked the driver. Habit impelled her to say Ireland and not America. She had got so sick of being treated like a tourist and asked if she was on holiday during the years she was living in Ireland that she'd become accustomed to saying she was from Galway. She hadn't got her head around her new – and old – identity yet, just as it hadn't yet sunk in that she was now a single entity. That's why she planned this trip to India; a three-month stopover – time to get strong enough to face a new life back home. The trip would be a buffer zone between her old life and her new one. The break-up would be far enough in the past by the time she arrived in California that no one would ask about it. All they would want to hear about would be the yoga and her new aura of wisdom and how she'd found herself in India.

'Island? What island?'

'Ireland,' she enunciated as well as she could, attempting to roll the R. The driver looked at her confused. In an effort to get him to face the windscreen again she added, 'It's next to England.'

'England! Yes! The queen?'

'Um, well . . .'

'Prince Charles?'

She let the driver list the names of the British royalty he knew until he petered out and as he did she tried to breathe and assimilate all that was challenging her senses. She felt very alone and helpless and tried to recreate the sense of empowerment she'd felt getting on the plane at Heathrow. If Fergus were here he'd talk to the driver; Fergus would chat to anyone. But Fergus wasn't here. Fergus was never up for any kind of big adventure. Never even went to the States with her because he couldn't get the money together for a flight. In three years. He could spend the rest of his life in his darkroom or wandering around fields with his camera.

Wow, a real shanty town, she thought as she saw from the taxi window cobbled-together shelters that looked like forts she used to build in her garden when she was a child. Then she spotted the first few people lying on the street, sleeping. The actual street. Because the pavements were full. First there were just a few but as they penetrated the city entire stretches of street were lined with the sleeping poor, side by side, some with blankets, some with cardboard, some with nothing. Children lay on windowsills and on power boxes. One old man was naked. She looked away, into the interior of the taxi again, at the beads hanging from the rear-view mirror and the coloured pictures of Hindu gods on the dashboard, at the photo of the Taj Mahal on the cover of her *Lonely Planet.*

Kristi looked up at the sign on the hotel they pulled up in front of and at the piece of paper in her hand. 'It's the wrong hotel,' she said to the driver, as she got out to stop him taking her rucksack out of the boot.

'This is the hotel of my friend. He will give you good price.'

'But—'

He was already marching into the foyer, carrying her rucksack. She followed him. He was at the desk booking her into a room. The man on reception handed the driver a few notes. The driver then turned to Kristi: '700 rupees, please'. She fiddled awkwardly with the flesh-coloured money belt that she had tucked into her waistband, conscious of being watched by the two men. She counted out notes and handed them to him. Why hadn't she negotiated the price before getting into the taxi, like the guidebook said? She was too weak to argue now. The driver took the notes, grinned at her, said, 'Welcome to India!' and was gone. The man on reception looked at her. 'What country?' he asked.

Kristi woke up and looked at the ceiling. For a few seconds she was newborn, had no idea where she was or when it was – she had been dreaming of her childhood bedroom in California and was disorientated not to awaken there, nor in her room in Ireland with Fergus beside her. She pulled the caul of mosquito net she'd draped over her before going to sleep from her face. An unmoving ceiling fan. Walls the colour of faded grass. She pulled the earplugs out of her ears and a thousand sounds came through the window and a hundred more from the other side of the door. She sat up and swivelled round, put her bare feet on the marble-like stone floor. Her knees were high as she sat on the edge of the low hard bed. Her heart beat fast as she looked around at the bare room. Her rucksack stared at her from a corner like an accusation. What had she been thinking coming to India by herself? She walked quietly to the window, as if afraid to alert anyone to her presence in case they might knock at the door, and pulled aside the flimsy curtain. On the street two storeys below flowed a messy river of people, battered cars, carts pulled by donkeys, rickshaws, some pulled by bicycles and some by the hands of scrawny men in sarongs and turbans. Carts selling fruit, cooking and selling food she did not recognise, a cow sidled along by itself, traffic parting either side of it, the women a moving prismatic kaleidoscope of saris, rubbish piled ankle deep where it had ended up at the edges of kerbs. She pulled the curtain to again, her heart palpitating. I can't go out there, she thought. I just can't. But I have to get out of here.

A shower would do her good; she always felt more able for life after a shower. She had been travelling for almost two days without washing. The bathroom was a pokey tiled room with a squat toilet and a tap about knee-high next to it, two plastic buckets, the large one full of water, the small one floating in it, a sink, and a shower fitting on the wall. She squatted awkwardly over the toilet and looked around for toilet paper that wasn't there. She brushed her teeth over the sink, using frugal drips from her bottle of water to do so. Then she switched on the shower and stood under it. The water was lukewarm, strange smelling and left a slimy residue on her skin. She began to sweat again almost immediately after stepping out from under it.

She dressed in zip-off cargo trousers and a top that she'd thought would be perfect for India, but she now realised their synthetic materials would be torture in the heat. She sat on the bed and ate the last sandwich from her carry-on bag, made with sliced pan, Kerrygold and red cheddar cheese. She brushed off the crumbs, picked up her *Lonely Planet*, took a deep breath and as she exhaled burst into passionate weeping between the pages on 'Indian Customs' and 'Mumbai Getting There and Getting Away'.

A knock at the door. She froze, but her chest heaved like a child's, gasping for air from crying so hard. Another knock. She quieted her breath and stared at the door willing her gaze to silence it. The handle turned. It was locked. 'Hello?' came a woman's voice from outside. A key in the lock. Turning. Kristi's heart hammered. A short woman in a green and purple sari with gold edging stepped into the doorway. She was old, though it was hard to tell how old – her hair was still black, bar a few strands of grey but her face was creased with the evidence of years. She had a broom in her hand. The woman said something in Hindi or some other language. Kristi looked at her and shrugged her shoulders. The woman made a sweeping motion with the broom and pointed into the room. Kristi said, 'It's okay. It doesn't need it,' and shook her head. The woman shook her head, or rather wobbled it from side to side on her neck, and proceeded into the room, sweeping with a smile that was at once meek and warm.

Kristi sat up on the bed against the wall and pulled her knees up to her chest. Her stomach felt like it was high in her torso. She held the book in her hands pretending to read. As the woman reached under the bed with her broom a few tears leaked out of Kristi. Then a sniffle. The woman looked at her and said

161

something in a concerned tone. Kristi tried to hold back but tears streamed down her cheeks. The woman sat on the bed and took her hand. She held it and whispered. Though the words meant nothing to Kristi, the susurrations had a comforting effect.

'Thank you,' she said to the woman after a while. The woman looked at the glossy cover picture of the Taj Mahal and smiled. She pointed to Kristi, the picture and back to Kristi again, with raised eyebrows. 'Oh no,' said Kristi. 'I don't think I'll make it there. I've made a big mistake.' The tears threatened to come again. She pointed to herself 'Kristi' and then to the woman, raised her eyebrows and repeated the sequence until the woman pointed to her and said 'Kriiisti' and then to herself, saying 'Shanti'. 'Shanti,' repeated Kristi. They both beamed at each other a moment. Then Shanti squeezed Kristi's hand and left the room, closing the door behind her.

Kristi lay on the bed, knocked supine by the heat and tiredness and alternated between closing her eyes and staring at the green walls for extended periods of time. More than anything or anyone in the world, she wanted Fergus there with her now. In the last few months she had come to think of him as useless but to just have him there would make her feel safe. He would deal with this. At the same time, she was so angry with herself for missing him, for wanting him there, for not being able to cope. She was supposed to be relieved to finally be free of him.

After what must have been a few hours it began to get dark; eventually the noise from the street died down and she dozed off. She woke again in darkness, her mouth parched. She reached for her water bottle and her heart sank to feel the bare weight of an empty plastic vessel as she picked it up. Outside her door was quiet. If she was ever going to venture outside her hotel room, then what better time to do it than in the middle of

162

the night. There might be a drink vending machine somewhere in the building. The corridor was quiet. When she reached the bottom of the stairs, she made out shapes on the floor of the lobby. The boy who had carried her rucksack to her room was lying on a mat on the hard floor, asleep alongside other boys who must work at the hotel too. She picked her way over them carefully. There was no vending machine anywhere in sight.

The next day when there was a knock at the door Kristi still said nothing but waited with bated breath. Shanti came in stooped and smiling. Kristi had the empty bottle and a bundle of rupees ready and brandished them with a desperation she could not conceal. If only Fergus could see her now. Shanti looked alarmed and understood. She took Kristi's hand and pulled it gently, turning in the direction of the door. Kristi resisted, like a two-year-old who does not want to get in a car. She held the bottle and the money out to Shanti, pushing them into the air in front of her and nodding at the woman. Shanti took the money and counted it. She clasped all of the fingertips of her empty right hand together and moved them towards her open mouth then pointed to Kristi. Kristi nodded and patted her stomach.

Kristi tried not to cry as she waited.

Shanti came back with a bag containing two bottles of water, one of which Kristi immediately imbibed half the contents of without touching the bottle to her lips, a bunch of tiny bananas, some mandarins; in her other hand she proffered a large flat round kind of pancake with a large dollop of yellowish sauce, served on a glossy banana leaf for a plate. 'Dosa,' said Shanti. Kristi rolled it up and devoured it. Shanti led her to the window and pointed just below on the street where a man was making dosas six at a time on a griddle on a cart.

Kristi's chest tightened at the sight of so many people and such chaos. Shanti picked up her broom and began sweeping.

Left alone again and with renewed energy and a sense of possibility Kristi looked through her paperwork – the photocopies of her tickets and insurance and phone numbers of family and friends she might need to contact. She had three copies of everything, spread between her money belt, her rucksack and her little bag. She thought about ringing Fergus, but what good would that do? She'd only end up crying down the phone and what could he do from another continent? Then she realised, her feeling of helplessness going into freefall, that even if she wanted to, she couldn't ring him. She no longer had a number for him since he'd moved out. All she had was his parents' number. She looked again at the name of the hotel she had intended to go to and her eyes teared up at the thought of another taxi ride that could end up anywhere.

Later that day there was another knock – panic subsided when she heard through the door 'Hello, Kristi' in Shanti's voice. Kristi sprang up and opened the door. Shanti was carrying two small paper cups. 'Chai,' she said, handing her one of the cups. Kristi was wary of drinking anything that hadn't come from a bottle, but it was steaming and looked like tea, so it must have been boiled. The sweet milky spiced tea was heaven – more comfort in a drink than Kristi could have imagined possible. She reached for her little purse, but Shanti shook her head.

'Thank you,' said Kristi. She thought of the boys sleeping on the floor and wondered where Shanti lived. They sat in silence and then Shanti stood up and left again, taking the empty cups with her. Kristi wanted to run after her and plead with her to stay a while. It was ridiculous, she knew. She heard the sound of Shanti's broom in the corridor outside, the soft rhythmic contact of straw against stone becoming quieter with distance until it faded out of earshot.

She awoke next morning to a banging on the door that penetrated her earplugs. 'Shanti?' she whispered, then repeated more loudly. 'Is that you, Shanti?'

'Madam?' came the voice of the man who had checked her in, presumably the owner. She pulled on her trousers and long-sleeved T-shirt and opened the door. 'Madam, you must kindly change rooms.'

'What? But—'

'This room is reserved. Please, you must go to different room.'

She scooped her toiletries and papers and the clothes she had unpacked back into her rucksack while he waited in the hallway. He beckoned her to follow and then waved her into a room with two bunk beds. Her instinct was to turn as soon as she saw the extra beds and walk back out, ask for a single room, but the man was gone and a head appeared from behind the bunk beds.

'Hi, I'm Ruth.' A girl a few years younger than Kristi, around twenty-five she guessed, held a tanned hand out to Kristi. The palm was webbed with fading intricate red designs. Kristi shook it.

'I'm Kristi,' she replied trying to take in the tangled beauty of the girl in front of her. Her skin was as deeply tanned as any white person's can be and her long wavy dark hair had dreadlocks in places which had little silver cuffs and coloured threads wrapped around them. It was all held back from her face with a patterned turquoise silk scarf. Her slight figure was swathed in coloured fabric that at once hid her body and draped from her shoulders and hips so as to accentuate its leanness.

'I'm Lucas,' came a voice from behind Kristi. She stepped aside and an equally tanned guy entered the room, around her own age she guessed, twenty-eight or so, with a tidy hair-cut, grown out a little and lightened in places by the sun. He was dressed in a maroon T-shirt and baggy pyjama-like trousers of faded multicoloured stripes. 'Are you hungry?' he said in a thick French accent. 'We are going out to get breakfast. Would you like to come with us?'

She walked half beside them, half in their wake, as they wove artfully through the streets. She kept her head down and watched their feet, so brown in their leather sandals. Ruth's silver anklets jangled as they walked. They seemed not to notice the people staring at them or the trail of beggar children they'd accumulated. The children chanted 'rupee, rupee' and tugged at the edges of their clothes. At each corner they turned they lost and gained different beggars, and rickshaw-wallahs shouted 'rickshaw, rickshaw' and 'what country?' at them.

'So where are you from?' Kristi asked Ruth. She hadn't been able to place her accent.

'I'm from Israel. I'm travelling for a year, or maybe two, depending on where I find work along the way. A lot of Israelis go travelling after their military service. I finished mine just before coming here. Lucas is from France.' They stepped around a naked toddler with something wrong with its abdomen laid across the pavement by its mother who held her hand out.

'Where are you from?' asked Ruth.

'Ireland.'

'Oh, but your accent? I thought you were American.'

166

'I've been living in Ireland for four years.' She found herself about to say 'Fergus, my boyfriend is Irish . . .' and stopped herself. How strange it was not to throw that into conversation at the beginning of a new acquaintanceship. It had always been such an important piece of establishing information, a way of placing herself in the world, in other people's eyes and estimation. She had not yet used the word ex in relation to him and couldn't bring herself to now. The thought of the word was shocking to her, let alone saying it out loud. She could say 'My boyfriend and I just split up' but who knows where that would lead. She really didn't want to be *that* girl.

They stopped at a shop that was little more than a kiosk in a wall and Lucas bought three bags of water, and handed one each to Ruth and Kristi, small square plastic bags they punctured at the corner and poured the contents straight into their mouths in one go. As they stood there an old woman whose eyes were misty with blindness said to Kristi, 'No rupees, just food.' Kristi looked to Ruth in panic. Ruth bought a packet of crackers from the kiosk and gave it to the woman, who thanked her with quiet fervour. They were gathering a small crowd. Kristi wanted to help them all. There were so many. There were too many.

The restaurant had the feel of a mess hall or canteen. The three of them sat in plastic chairs at a Formica table. Ruth and Lucas took a cursory glance at the laminated menu while Kristi stared at it, her eyes zigzagging all over it. 'I don't know what any of these things are,' she answered when Ruth asked if she knew what she wanted to order. 'That's a good thing,' said Lucas. 'I have had so many banana pancakes for breakfast here I don't know if I could look at another one.'

'Anyway,' added Ruth, 'it's best to get something properly Indian into your system. They can tell you've just arrived by the smell of your sweat.'

'Here, this is a good choice to try.' Lucas pointed at 'Thali' on the menu.

'Okay,' said Kristi lightly, feeling almost upbeat for the first time since she arrived, and Ruth put in the order.

'So, how long are you staying in India?' Lucas asked.

'Well, my plan was three months, but I might leave sooner.'

'Three months is nothing! You are only getting to know a place after three months. I've been here six months and I could see a new place every day if I stayed another six.'

'He's right,' said Ruth, 'I've been here four and a half months and I had only planned to come for two.'

'Did you know each other before you came here?'

They laughed.

'No,' said Lucas. 'We met in Goa.'

'The first week I arrived,' added Ruth. 'Then we met up again in Varanasi and in Darjeeling and then we decided to just travel together.'

So, this is what everyone said about making friends along the way. Now she would have someone to travel with, too. She could just fit in with whatever travel plans they had and she'd be okay. It would mean being a third wheel but that was better than being on her own.

'So where are you headed after here?' she asked, ready to go wherever they were going.

'Oh, we fly out first thing tomorrow,' said Lucas. 'We were both going to Australia next anyway, so we arranged to fly on the same day.' He gave Ruth the kind of soft look that reminded Kristi of her new and chosen status of being single.

She felt the safety net she had just discovered falling out from under her and Mumbai closed around her again.

'Where are you going?' Lucas asked her.

'I haven't quite decided yet.'

'Oh, go to Goa!' said Ruth.

'Yes, it is paradise,' said Lucas. 'White beaches, blue sea. There are really cool little restaurants on the beaches and cliffs.'

'Yes, it is the perfect place to go when you have just arrived,' said Ruth. 'You can get used to the heat there and the food and get a tan so that you look like you have not just stepped off a plane.'

A man came out from behind the counter and delivered their food: three metal trays and on them flat, round breads and small metal bowls with different contents: a few with curry-like substances in varying shades of yellow, brown and green, and one with what looked like natural yoghurt. Then he placed a metal beaker full of water in front of each of them. Kristi went to pick hers up. She was thirsty again already. Lucas put his hand over hers to stop her and widened his eyes.

'Oh yes, I forgot,' said Kristi.

She waited for the cutlery to arrive. Ruth, using just her right hand, tore off a strip of bread and holding it in her bunched fingertips, scooped sauce onto it and got it into her mouth as if her hand was the beak of a giant bird. Lucas did the same. Everyone in the place was doing the same and with incredible speed. Ruth laughed a kind laugh. 'You get used to it in no time.'

Kristi thought she knew what curry was until then. She thought she knew what spicy was. But everything was spicy, bar the yoghurt which the others informed her was called curd. It was soothing relief between the burning mouthfuls of everything else.

It was hard to believe that only two weeks ago she'd had her last breakfast with Fergus. Why had he not begged her to stay when she'd left with her suitcase that evening? Why hadn't he dropped to his knees and promised to change and proposed to her? She'd gone to a friend's place for a few nights to give him time to move out – and that's exactly what he did. When she came back he and his stuff were gone. He hadn't left a note – or any money for bills for that matter. The only thing on the kitchen table was her favourite mug, which looked like he'd broken and then repaired it. There'd been no word from him. No phone call or letter. There was nothing holding her back from living her dreams any more. She could prove that she was still as independent and brave as she had been before she'd met Fergus. Before her life had become merged with his, back when she was whole and not somebody's other half. This was all his fault. But watching this new couple – were they a couple? – opposite her, she wanted him there beside her. She wanted him there so that she could say 'A couple of months is nothing! You're not even getting to know each other yet! You don't know what a real relationship is, one that lasts for years. Not some silly travelling romance.'

She tried her best to shelter between them as they wound back through the streets to the hotel. There had been some respite from the quotidian mayhem of the streets of Mumbai while they'd been in the restaurant as the beggars and touts were kept out, but now she felt it again, assaulting her senses. It was an effort to keep herself together. She breathed deeply to stop herself from being shattered into tiny pieces by the things she saw. Doing her best to act like all of this was normal she caught it all in glances, thinking it rude to stare. A cluster of children and adults covered with minimal clothing made their daily ablutions at a street pump – the old-fashioned kind of hand pump with a long handle – filling plastic buckets, soaping themselves all over and then rinsing the lather, brushing their teeth, one child squatting over a grated drain, defecating into it.

They stopped at another kiosk. Kristi gave Ruth money to get some things for her. As Ruth was paying for fruit, crackers, biscuits and water, Kristi picked up a bar of whitening soap, a picture of a dubiously pale-looking Indian woman's face on it. Lucas smiled at her confused expression as she turned the box over in her hand. 'Funny, isn't it?' he said, smiling. 'And we are all out in the sun trying to get brown. Humans are crazy, no? Never happy with what they have.'

They passed a cinema, its huge billboards displaying hand-painted movie posters, one for *Shaft* with Samuel L. Jackson (spectacular action thriller!) and one for *Life is Beautiful* (winner 3 Academy Awards). Above the posters was 'Now Showing' with 'Enjoy Coca-Cola' either side of it. An elephant sidled through the traffic, its sides painted with designs and a script of sweeping lines and curlicues, a man sitting on top of a railed platform for a driver's seat. A woman on the street put a coin in the elephant's trunk; it threw the coin up to its owner up top, then the woman bowed her head and the elephant touched its trunk to the crown of it. Others gathered to do the same. The women all had shining black hair in plaits. Some had bindis, and some had coloured powder in the parting of their hair.

Kristi couldn't help thinking of all the photographs that could be taken, of how Fergus would gorge himself on these sights if he were here. To see all of this without him felt like she was not fully experiencing it, like there was no point in being here if she could not share it; she couldn't even tell him about it.

The heat had intensified and it pushed down on Kristi's head like a weight. All the way back to the hotel her feet slid in her new sandals, the straps rubbed at her heels, working steadily to form blisters. She wanted to take off her long-sleeved black and grey T-shirt which felt like a wool blanket and walk around in the pretty white vest top underneath, but Ruth told her she had to keep her arms, her shoulders covered. Ruth in the opaque, coloured top that floated like gossamer, Ruth with the silk scarf protecting her head. And the beggars kept coming, kept hounding, little children, why weren't they in school? Adorable faces, looking at her with practised brown puppy-dog eyes, following them when they crossed the street to get away from them and the men saying you want rickshaw, you want hotel, you want rickshaw, you want hotel, you want rickshaw, you want hotel, and the man missing both legs sitting on the pavement among the rubbish and dirt and the smells of incense and spices and refuse, and dogs that looked like balding coyotes nosing the debris, and the horns beeping beeping beeping, various music coming from various buildings and cars, and the ox-drawn carts and the hundreds of mopeds buzzing, the shops the width of doorways crowded side by side, wooden fronts, pulled open baring goods: dry foods, rice, lentils, chickpeas, coloured powders, old-fashioned scales with weights, cobblers, dressmakers, fruit and vegetables, buckets of fish, all of the signs written in Hindi and in English, a cow sticking its nose into a shop, shooed out by the owner . . . and finally the hotel. The cool shade of it. The cool stone floor. The familiar face of the man on reception greeting them.

On the way up the stairs they passed Shanti who was sweeping it down. Kristi stopped to say hello and was struck dumb with the frustration of having no words in common with her, having spent the morning chatting freely to Lucas and Ruth. Shanti gave her a broad smile and pointed to the two who were going on ahead as if to say, 'Look you have friends now who are like you', and it suddenly occurred to Kristi that the room change could have been Shanti's doing. She blushed for a moment with the thought that she had been so vulnerable in front of her and then she took her hand and smiled with gratitude.

Back in the room Lucas sat on one of the bottom bunks and rolled a joint. 'It's called charas here, by the way, in case you are going to buy some,' he said. Kristi nodded and climbed the ladder to the top bunk of the bed Ruth was sitting on the bottom of, opposite Lucas. She propped her head on her folded arms at the edge so they could all see each other. Lucas passed Ruth the joint and after a few drags she passed it up to Kristi, who, not knowing how to say no and still be their friend, took two drags and passed it back down to Lucas on the opposite bed.

'Goa. Yeah, that's got to be your first stop,' he said dreamily and lay on his back on the bed, one arm folded behind his head. 'We stayed in this great place – it's just like little bungalows of individual rooms built all over a hill by the cliff. I'll write down the name for you.'

'Hey, why don't you share a taxi with us in the morning?' said Ruth, swivelling her head to look up from where she was perched on the bunk under Kristi. 'We can drop you off at the

173

train station on our way. You need to get there early to get your ticket.'

'That would be great, thank you,' said Kristi and she heard a whisper of the 'I'm doing it' thought she'd had on the plane rise in her.

'Are you going to Darjeeling? You have to go to Darjeeling,' said Lucas. 'It was my favourite place here. You can get a jeep up Tiger Hill to see the sunrise illuminate the Himalayas. It's the most beautiful thing I've ever seen. With the snow on the mountains, the pink morning light – it looks like strawberry and vanilla ice-cream . . . Ruth, can you give me the biscuits, please.'

Ruth held the joint up for Kristi to take and then rummaged in the plastic bag for biscuits which she passed across to Lucas who continued talking while opening the packet.

'Of course you have to go to Agra to see the Taj Mahal. Oh, and Varanasi is amazing, too! I mean it's total chaos but it is beautiful chaos, with wedding processions going through the streets and the brides and grooms, all the jewellery and make-up are fascinating to see, and then there are the funeral pyres burning at the side of the Ganges – it's like life and death and everything in between comes together there and you can go for a boat ride on the river at sunset.'

'If you go there stay in the Yogi Lodge,' said Ruth. 'But make sure the taxi driver brings you to the real Yogi Lodge. There are other fake ones that copied the name just to get business. Make sure you have the address.'

'That's kind of how I ended up here – the taxi driver just brought me here even though I asked to go to a different one.'

'Same with us, but we couldn't be bothered going through the hassle of arguing with him for our last night.'

174

'Yeah, we thought, let him have his commission. What do we care? It's not like we need to meet other backpackers when we're leaving for Australia tomorrow anyway,' said Lucas then paused for a moment. 'Oh, and Pondicherry if you're going south, yeah, you gotta go there, too. It's a really chilled place. You can even rent bikes and cycle around there. There's this ashram you can visit called Auroville.'

'It does get quite hot down south,' said Ruth.

The pair regaled Kristi with stories from their travels and advice for where she should go, how they found an ohm-shaped beach without road access where you could stay in a mud-hut for only 35 rupees, and a guy named Krishna who gave them a chillum pipe to smoke and taught them to play bridge, about how they'd spent thirty-six hours on a train from Chennai to Kolkata, and about giant banyan trees and sunsets and sunrises and stomach issues and temples and all the Hindu gods they could name. Kristi did her best to take it all in, but her head was swimming after the smoke. She withheld her questions about what certain words meant but panicked inside desperately trying to remember them in case they were important. Banyan, chillum, Kali . . .

'Are you coming with us?' Lucas's face hovered beside Kristi's. She had been away in a dream-like state. He was standing beside the bunk.

'We're going to do some shopping,' Ruth informed her, 'for things that are cheaper here than in Australia.'

'Oh, no thanks,' said Kristi. 'I think I'll stay here and plan my journey.'

'Okay, see you later.'

'Au revoir!' said Lucas cheerily, pulling the door behind them.

It was quiet again in the room – or at least the only sounds now were coming from outside. Kristi's body felt like lead but she needed to pee. And she was starving. Those biscuits had only whetted her appetite. She spent what felt like a very long time psyching herself up to climb down, and when she did she moved like a ninja in slow motion in case anyone would hear the creak of the bed or the sound of her bare feet on the floor. She turned the doorknob of the en-suite with the precision of someone breaking into a safe. When she pulled the cord for the light, she was sure she saw something scurry and disappear into the ceramic hole of the squat toilet. Was it a cockroach? She leaned the top half of her body over to see. Nothing. But she'd definitely seen something. Hadn't she? She was really stoned. She peed as quickly as she could and then used the little bucket to rinse the way Ruth had told her Indians do instead of using toilet paper. The bucket was the size of ones she'd used to make sandcastles when she was a child. On beaches where there were no dead bodies. Lucas had told her that dead bodies wash up on the beach in Mumbai.

Having made her way stealthily back onto the top bunk, clutching a packet of biscuits, she lay and exhaled deeply. The ordeal was over. Then she lay her hand by her side and touched the guidebook. Her insides sank. She should read up on Goa at least. Make a plan. Her body was so heavy though and her mind scrambled; she couldn't pick up the book, let alone read. Sleep would be a relief but her mind wasn't about to let her do that either.

She remembered a friend of hers saying after a break-up that she felt like one of her arms had been cut off. Kristi hadn't understood it at the time and even now she was aware that all her limbs were intact, but a part of her was definitely missing. Who even was she if she wasn't Fergus's girlfriend? How easy it had been to deflect attention away from herself with the statement 'My boyfriend is a photographer.' She'd hadn't needed to prove herself; she could define herself by him, she could be interesting by association. Who was she now? Not the daring, independent person she thought she would be without him.

A knock at the door. Shanti's voice saying hello through it. Another knock. The squeak of the knob turning. Kristi lay completely still. She couldn't talk to her in this state. To anyone. She'd pretend to be asleep. Or Shanti might just not see her at all. The rhythmic sweeping began. With her eyes closed Kristi could not tell whether the sweeping was near her or on the other side of the room. The sweeping stopped. Did she look like she was asleep? Maybe she didn't look asleep. Was she breathing like someone who was asleep? She'd never seen herself asleep so how could she know? She took an extra deep breath just to be sure. What if Shanti spoke to her and she had to say something – she wouldn't be able to because her mouth was too dry. That was ridiculous, though – they didn't even speak the same language. How could she talk to her? Maybe Shanti hadn't even seen her at all. There was a rustling sound. Maybe she – maybe she was robbing them. All the rucksacks were down below on the floor. If they got robbed it would be Kristi's fault. At least she had her passport on her in her money belt. The sweeping started again. It continued all the way out the door and then the door clicked shut. Shanti's footsteps faded.

Kristi opened her eyes and looked down at the rucksacks. They all seemed to be in order. She felt awful for pretending to be asleep when Shanti was there but what else could she do? She took a swig of water from the bottle beside her pillow and then did actually sleep for a while, a deep and peaceful sleep. By the time she woke to the sound of the others coming in she was feeling normal again. She turned on her side and propped herself up on one elbow to say hello to them. They shook out plastic bags onto their beds and showed her boxes and boxes of incense, essential oils, soaps, packets of bindis, oil burners made from carved soapstone. Ruth had bought a sari the colour of turmeric and a huge silver pendant.

'You wouldn't believe how much the guy was asking for this necklace! Seriously, it was like Western prices. In the end I began to walk away and he gave it to me for a quarter of what he'd asked for.'

'This girl knows how to haggle,' said Lucas.

Kristi could get her head around conversion rates – she still converted pounds to dollars in her head all the time – and her mental arithmetic was sharp for adding taxes and tips, but the idea of not knowing the price of something and having to guess it without insulting the seller or getting ripped off was awful. She just wanted the prices to be on everything.

'How are your travel plans going?' asked Lucas.

'Oh good, good. I was just reading about Goa,' said Kristi.

Ruth and Lucas took everything out of their rucksacks and laid it out on their respective beds so they could pack properly for Australia. Kristi leaned over to watch them, praying Shanti hadn't stolen anything.

The three of them left the hotel in a taxi in the early hours of the morning. The others had booked it through the

178

reception. They settled a price with the driver before they got in. The city, bathed in orange street light, was easing into day. Lucas hopped in the front and Ruth and Kristi sat in the back.

'I can't believe my time in India is over already,' said Ruth, 'but at the same time it feels like I've been here for ever.' There was an air of nostalgia about her voice and she seemed to be looking out of the window, taking everything in for one last time. 'And you have it all ahead of you!'

Kristi mustered as much of a smile as she could and said, 'You must be excited about Australia?'

Ruth's face lit up. 'Oh, yes! Ever since I was a child I have wanted to go there. This time tomorrow . . .' She gave a little squeal of excitement.

'No more easy life then, Ruthie,' chimed in Lucas from the front seat. He had been chatting to the driver but tuned into their conversation. 'We will have to work there.'

'Yes, we're going to look for work and maybe stay in one place for a while to save some money,' Ruth informed Kristi. 'But I'm looking forward to a bit of stability – for a little while anyway.'

There was a silence. Kristi felt cocooned in the taxi. Then Ruth, who had become contemplative, said, 'You know what it is? I've loved it here. But I am ready to move on now.'

'Yes,' agreed Lucas. 'I know what you mean. I'm sure I will come back here someday. But now I am ready to move on.'

The taxi pulled up outside the train station, a huge building of ornate architecture with archways into it. Kristi took a deep breath and got out of the car. Lucas and Ruth got out, hugged her goodbye, then got back into the taxi and disappeared into the traffic.

She stood with her rucksack at her feet. From where she was she could see through an archway into the station. A wide mob-like queue swelled and swayed in through the archway to the bottom of a wide staircase signposted 'Tickets'. She stood, unmoving, looking at it. She seemed to have brought with her a layer of the cocoon from the taxi. The volume seemed turned down around her. Beggars bounced off it. Of all the things fighting for the attention of her senses, none of them got it fully. She had the feeling of being in a daydream into which the world could not fully intrude.

Suddenly the swarm that waited for tickets began to jostle as the stairway was opened and a small stampede was held in check by security guards with batons who herded the people like cattle and whacked those trying to circumnavigate the 'queue'.

'Madam, there is a separate queue for tourists,' a man dressed in a suit, who had evidently seen her look of horror and confusion, said to her and continued on his way.

'What country?' another man said to her. 'You want taxi? Hotel?'

She could take a taxi to a shop on the way back to the hotel and stock up on dry food goods and water. Shanti would help her find a telephone and she would call USIT and get them to change the date of her flight to San Francisco to as soon as possible. She would sit out the few days she had to wait in the hotel. She would pay Shanti for helping her. She would spend her time in quiet meditation and find inner peace. She would stop dreaming about Fergus, stop thinking about him. She would be ready to move on. That is what she would say to herself in the taxi on the way to the airport in a few days, that her time in India was valuable, that she might come back one day, but that now she was ready to move on.

The seats are three across. None of the windows have glass, just bars. Opposite her sits a couple with a little girl. The man has a thick moustache and wears brown trousers and a blue and white check shirt, the woman is younger than him and very beautiful, wearing a cerise sari and a gold nose ring that is connected by a delicate chain to her ear. She has red powder in the parting of her hair. The little girl has short hair and is wearing a skirt and T-shirt with a picture of flowers on it and she has a gold bangle around each wrist. To Kristi's side is an empty seat between her and an older lady who seems to be with the couple opposite. She feels all of their eyes on her, though she has to admit she is entranced by how they look, too.

She stands up and reaches into the side pocket of her rucksack which is lying down in an overhead rack. She pulls out her guidebook. There is something else underneath it in the pocket. She pulls out a long string of dimpled red beads the size of hazelnuts. They are light; they appear to be some sort of dried seeds. She'd seen a string like this in the taxi from the airport, hanging from the rear-view mirror. So that's what Shanti had been doing: leaving her a present. Kristi's stomach shrinks – to think she'd thought Shanti was stealing from them. She puts the necklace on and sits down with her book in her lap.

The young woman opposite is looking at Kristi's neck. She points. 'You have mala,' she says.

'Mala?'

'Yes,' says the young woman. 'They give protection to the traveller.'

'Oh.'

'They bring peace,' she adds and smiles.

'They are prayer beads,' says the man. 'Made of rudraksha seeds.'

'Thank you. I didn't know that,' she says to her fellow passengers. 'They were a gift from a friend.'

With a judder the train moves off. As it does a young woman around Kristi's age with a rucksack plonks into the seat next to her. Her skin is as white as china and her blue eyes stand out from her jet-black hair. 'Hi,' she says nervously to Kristi.

'Hi. You going to Goa?'

'Yes. You?'

'Yep. You know what village you're going to?' asks Kristi.

'Well, I think Arambol.'

'That's where I'm heading too. I met a couple who gave me the name of a place to stay.'

'Oh.'

'Maybe we could go find this place together? If you like?'

'That would be fantastic. To be honest I'm a bit freaked out. I only arrived yesterday. How long have you been here?'

'A few days. I got delayed in Mumbai, but I'm ready to move on now.'

There was a silence between them for a moment. Then the girl whispered, 'I dyed my hair to come here because a friend told me I'd be stared at if I was blonde. I don't think it's done any good.'

'I think we might just have to get used to it,' said Kristi. 'I'm Kristi, by the way.'

'Oh, sorry, I'm Satu.'

The doors of the train remain open all the time. People run after the train and jump on from the tracks as it pulls away from stations. At one station a young man with a metal tank, something like a Burco boiler strapped to his back, gets on and makes his way down the aisle calling 'Chai, chai, chai! Chai, chai, chai!' Passengers rummage in their pockets and purses for coins. Kristi does, too. 'Two,' she says to the wallah when he reaches their seat. She gives him the same amount as everyone else has been paying and he fills one little paper cup and hands it to her, then another. She gives one to Satu.

'What's this?' asks Satu.

'The most comforting drink in the world,' answers Kristi.

The family across from them also get chai. The little girl giggles at Satu tasting the drink with suspicion and then delight. The man lowers his cup for a moment and says to them, 'What country are you from?'

'Finland,' answers Satu.

'America,' says Kristi.

She sips in the spices and tea and milk and sugar and leans her head back against the hard headrest and lets the warm wind stroke her face, like dry sheets flapping on a summer clothes' line. The countryside moves by like a slide show. Huts roofed with plaited palm leaves, coconut trees, goat-herds walking their goats along rail tracks, cotton-fields, a scarecrow wearing a turban, rice paddies dotted with brightly dressed women crouching and bending to pick crops, mountains, sugarcane, people washing clothes in rivers and laying them in the sun to dry.

Your Body, Dolores

When you are nineteen you will lie on a table and let a man cut you. You will love this man so much that you will do anything for him. You will let him change your shape in all sorts of ways, and all of your own free will. Time will move you towards him, inevitably. The night you meet him you will buoy yourself up with a line of cocaine before entering the swanky London hotel function room. You will plunge elegantly through the crowds, eyes outlined in kohl, your long red hair billowing behind you with the silk of your floor-length emerald-green dress. The band will be playing 'Hotel California'. He will appear before you, a short balding man, and he will say to you something cheesy like 'What's a pretty girl like you doing at this stuffy do?' You won't care what he thinks; the coke will have emboldened you. 'I'm here for the free booze,' you will say, hoping to shock him. You will look down at him and think that you know so much more than he does because you will have been on the road four years already at that point. All he knows is books, you will think. And money. He will say, 'Here you go, Doll,' and hand you a glass of champagne, making you feel like a Hollywood movie star. You will forget the vow you made when leaving home in the middle of the night, the vow to never let anyone make you do things you don't want to do. But what of it? You will already have forgotten sincere vows to never smoke or drink or do drugs. You will look around for someone else to talk to at the party, but he will keep asking you questions and you will stay and talk to him because you will know that is your job. You and the other actors, the musicians, the performers, have been invited to entertain this sea of tweed suits. You know that the free booze and food comes at a price. He will say something that will make you laugh and you will think this guy's not that bad. He will ask you about actors and the difference between them and celluloid artists and you will tell him of the depths of humanity Andy Warhol reaches into. Henry, for you will know his name by then, will confide that he has always wanted to be an artist but that there had been a tradition of doctors in his family. 'With my fine motor skills,' he will say, 'it would have been a crime not to become a surgeon.' You will laugh at this. Then he will say that he was named after Henry Grey and you will not know whether to admit you have no clue who Henry Grey is but he will kindly explain before you have to ask that he was a famous surgeon who wrote the book *Grey's Anatomy*. 'Do you know how much he achieved in his life?' he will ask. No, you don't. 'And he died at the age of thirty-four,' he will say, 'I'm six years older than that already!' You should think, 'He is so old!' But you won't. You will see how his family's expectations still rile him and you will want to soothe him. You will want to take his side. You will want to encourage the artist in him. You will think you understand him better than anyone else in this room, or anyone else in his life. You will feel a heady buzz and will let everything around you fall away but Henry, as if a camera is doing a three hundred and sixty around you both. You will let him put his hand on the small of your back and you will like the way it warms the cool silk against your skin. You will go home with him and you will leave the old Dolores with all her teenage vows, standing at the party, a shed skin.

For ten years Henry will sculpt you. He will draw dotted lines on your body that will remind you of the paper cut-out dolls you had as a child. The first time he does it you will giggle and tell him it tickles. He will have you anaesthetised, put a scalpel underneath your breasts and open them like gills. He will make them bigger and sew them up. He will peel back the skin from your nose and file away bone, adjust the cartilage. He will stretch the skin on your face to keep it smooth and taut. He will fatten your lips. He will make your breasts bigger and bigger. He will give you pills for the pain and will hire the best tailors to engineer brassieres for you. He will take you to be his wife and to all the fancy functions and you will feel like a Bond Girl.

When you are twenty-nine and Henry is fifty he will return one day to your home on Richmond Green with a tabloid in hand; the front page will bear a picture of you and him under the headline 'Britain's biggest boobs'. 'Forget it,' you'll say. 'They don't understand.' You will invite him to sit on the three-seater sofa and you will rub his back. You won't say any more because you will know his ways by then. But he will not forget it.

He will ask you to stay indoors when he is at work. You will do this for him. You will start to want to have a baby.

The longing will grow stronger with every day alone in the house. You will want to love a child like you were never loved. When you tell him this, he will offer to buy you a dog. He will remind you that years ago you both agreed never to have children. You will say 'Look at me' and he will look at you – at your short permed hair, your pink lipgloss and blush, your hot pink dress with the padded shoulders and the sweetheart neckline – 'I am not the same girl I was when I met you. I have been your Plasticine, your living sculpture. I deserve this one thing.' You will be shaking when you say this, because you will be feeling strong and terrified at the same time. He will say he is too old to be a father. He will say he's not sure your body can handle it. When your eyes well up, he will say, 'All right, Doll, but I'll have to loosen the skin around your abdomen first.' You will be so tired of operations, of anaesthetics, of waiting to be finished, of waiting to heal.

In the small hours you will begin to think about the night you left home at fifteen and all the vows you made to yourself then. You will want a normal life. You will agree to this one last surgery. When you come round after it you will feel odd. He will come and see you in the recovery room as usual and, though your vision will be blurred, he will seem to avoid eye contact when he kisses your forehead. When you are back home alone a few days later, you will stand and look out of the window at children kicking piles of fallen leaves on the green. You will touch your hand to your stomach and it will not feel looser on the outside. Instead it will feel tighter inside, as if someone had tied a double blood knot in there.

Aperture

As you get better at taking photographs, you might find you want to invest in more lenses for your camera so you can broaden the scope of the kinds of pictures you take. It is worth getting a good one – they are expensive, but if you are patient and look around there are good lenses to be bought second-hand.

Bringing a stranger back to his house was something James would never normally do, but the young Irishman had been friendly to him in a way no one had in such a long time. He slipped the key in the front door, hesitated for a moment, and then led the way. Fergus followed him in, wiping his feet on the mat, tightening his grip on the shoulder straps of the backpack he was wearing. One like those the college students carry their books in, James had thought as they'd walked to the house. Those casual chats with strangers, comments on the weather and so forth, just didn't happen these days, not since Rose's Tearoom had become a Starbucks and all the

188

people in it turned to automatons, welded to their phones and laptops. It was so refreshing to have someone ask did he mind if they joined him, to talk idly about the newspaper headlines and joke about the gargantuan size of the cups and saucers.

James led Fergus through the hallway, immaculately kept with its gold-coloured carpet, mahogany telephone seat and umbrella stand, and into the sitting room. Truth be told, Fergus reminded him a little of Ben, though Ben was probably a bit older than Fergus. And when he'd mentioned to Fergus the bother he'd been having with his computer, it seemed natural to accept the help he offered, to let him pop round and take a quick look, see if it wasn't something simple he could fix.

As they entered the sitting room, James's father's clock – the one the telegram office had given him on his retirement – on the mantelpiece gave four tiny gongs. He watched Fergus's eyes be drawn to the clock and linger on the silver-framed photo of Tegan next to it. Tegan at thirty. Tegan, forever thirty in James's mind. Sometimes he tried to imagine her face like his, having wrinkled with time and her hair gone grey, but an image of her like that refused to form.

As Fergus's gaze finally broke away from Tegan and he scanned the room, James became acutely aware of how old-fashioned and cluttered the place was. The dining table was covered with stamp albums, and several open cardboard boxes of Tegan's clothes lined the wall beside it.

'Please excuse the mess,' he said. 'I've been having a bit of a clear-out.'

'Not at all,' said Fergus. 'A mess makes me feel at home!'

'Oh you're very kind. You'd be amazed at how much fits in an attic. I've been selling what things I can and donating the rest to charity shops. Well, here's the computer.'

Fergus put his backpack down on the floor, leaning it against a leg of the table and patting it, as if making sure its contents were still there. James sat at the small desk in the corner and wriggled the mouse about until the screen came on. 'See, this won't close, and I can't seem to open anything else. It's all stuck.'

'I see,' said Fergus. James stood and moved aside to let Fergus at the computer.

'Could you handle another cup of tea?' James asked. He was enjoying the company and didn't want it to end.

'Absolutely,' answered Fergus enthusiastically as he held down some keys and the screen went blank.

In the kitchen James assembled a tea tray and waited for the kettle to boil. Maybe clearing out the attic had something to do with this new self. Maybe that's what made him act out of character and bring a stranger into his house. He was feeling a sense of renewal lately, though he suspected this was somehow ironically linked to his gradual acceptance of his own mortality. Turning seventy had nudged him towards reflection.

When James went back into the sitting room to clear a space on the table, Fergus was facing away from the computer, staring at the photo of Tegan. James cleared his throat. Fergus swung around to face him.

'It's all working fine again,' he said.

James looked at the glowing screen behind Fergus.

'Fantastic. Thank you so much. Let me give you a few bob for that.'

'Not at all! All I did was shut it down and restart it. A cup of tea will do fine.'

James lifted a stack of albums from the dining table and placed them on the floor beside the boxes. 'Stamps,' he explained. 'I've been collecting since I was a boy. That's the main thing I use the computer for. For finding collectors and using websites like eBay. Especially since so many of the smaller stamp clubs have been closing. We're a dying breed.'

He did use the computer for email, too. He thought it would be a good way to stay in touch with Ben, but it seemed Ben was as averse to emailing as he was to making phone calls. It must have been nearly two years since James had seen him. It was bad enough when Ben had been living in London but since he'd moved to Wales he may as well have emigrated to Australia.

Fergus moved over towards the stack of albums. 'Do you mind if I have a look?'

'Please do.' James extended his arm. 'It's not often anyone shows an interest.'

He went into the kitchen and brought out the tray on which sat two steaming mugs of tea, a plate of digestives, a china jug of milk and a sugar bowl. He put it on the table and Fergus, having perused the top album and replaced it on the stack, sat down at the dining table, poured milk into one of the mugs and picked up a biscuit. James noticed Fergus's line of sight was now directed straight ahead at a framed photo on the sideboard of Tegan with Ben, as a toddler, on her lap.

James cleared more space by lifting a shoebox off the table. It was full of letters, addressed to 'James Deane with an E'. They were the only letters he had left from when he worked in the sorting office, back when he used to steal letters from time to time. Just for their stamps. He'd always intended on sending the letters on later. And this year, when he'd found boxes of the stolen letters in the attic, he'd felt so ashamed of himself that he had finally done that. He wanted to make amends, so over a few months he had put the decades-old letters into new envelopes and posted them from various pillar boxes, under the cover of night. He imagined all those letters arriving so many years late. If only he could receive a letter, a message, a sign from Tegan, he would be so relieved, even if it was years late. Only yesterday he had delivered the last letter. It was the first one he'd taken. The stamp would have only ended up in the bin if he hadn't helped himself to it. He knew it would have because the letter was addressed to Nigel Bennett and Nigel knew nothing about stamps.

Nigel, who had pretended to be his friend but was cruel to him when they were young. He still saw him around the town sometimes and they saluted each other, nothing more. Nigel had married and divorced twice – for all his bravado, he never had much luck with women.

Fergus bit into his biscuit and chewed loudly. He was looking at the boxes of Tegan's clothes.

'They're my wife's,' said James.

'Oh.'

'She's been gone twenty-seven years now.'

Fergus looked at his tea.

'Her clothes are good for nothing but fancy dress now. Seems silly to hold on to something so long, doesn't it?'

'No,' said Fergus. 'Not at all.' He paused and then said, 'My girlfriend just left me – I'm sorry I don't know why I said that.'

'You must miss her,' said James, smoothing over Fergus's embarrassment.

'I do.'

'I still miss my Tegan every day.'

'How did she die, if you don't mind me asking?'

'Oh, she didn't die. She went out for a walk one day and never came back. Just vanished.'

'Jesus.'

They both fell silent for a moment, looking at the boxes of clothes. A shiny lemon-yellow dress sat at the top of one, a pair of grass-green cords at the top of another.

'Did you ever have a beard?' asked Fergus.

James looked at him, searching his expression for the intention behind the odd question and finding nothing answered, 'No. Why do you want to know that?'

'I have to tell you something,' said Fergus. He inhaled deeply. 'I didn't just happen to be in that coffee shop. I followed you there.'

James put his mug down and pulled his body back in his chair. So this is how it ends. This is why you don't bring strangers into your house.

'Oh no, don't worry. I'm not going to harm you or anything. It's just, I had your address, but I didn't know how to . . .' He exhaled deeply, placed his mug on the table, leaned down and picked up his backpack.

James held his breath. The telephone was too far away, and he could never outrun this young man. Fergus unzipped the backpack and pulled out a slim cardboard box, a bit bigger than foolscap and handed it to James. It said Ilford photographic paper on it.

'What is this?' asked James as he hesitatingly took it.

'I bought a lens from you on eBay about two months ago.'

'Tegan's lens. Yes, I remember posting it to Ireland. That was you who bought it? But how did you . . . what are you . . . did you travel all the way here to find me?'

'Open the box.'

With shaking hands James took the lid off the box. It was full of photographs. The top one was of Nigel Bennett in what looked like the early seventies, in a mustard jumper, on his face a still-black beard and a wide grin, standing in front of a fishing pole, the lake in the background.

'What . . .' James looked from the box of photos to Fergus. 'That's not you, is it?'

'No, it's not. Where did you get these?' He lifted the photo of Nigel and looked at the one underneath it. Tegan in white flares and a turquoise blouse, leaning towards the camera in a Marilyn pose, blowing a kiss. A kick to his gut. 'Tell me, where did you get these?'

'I took them, I mean the lens took them. I know it sounds crazy. That's why I had to come and find you and show you.'

'What do you mean, the lens took them?' James shuffled through the photos in the box as best he could. Then he stood up, cleared away the tea tray and another two shoeboxes. He tipped the photos out onto the centre of the table, spreading them out like jigsaw pieces.

'The lens I bought from you. When I started using it, these sort of . . . ghost images started appearing over whoever I was photographing. They got stronger with every roll of film until . . . well, now these are the only photos my camera will take when I use that lens, no matter what I point it at.'

'Tegan's lens.' James began to cry at the images splayed out in front of him. All of them taken at the lake. Tegan in seductive poses, close-ups of Nigel's face, then one of the two of them – slightly off-centre, Tegan sitting on Nigel's lap on his fishing stool – in which they are kissing.

'I'm sorry,' said Fergus. 'I don't know what they mean. I just got this feeling I had to show you, so I got in the car and got on a ferry and . . . I thought it might make sense to you.'

'My Tegan . . . and Nigel. He never . . . they never—'

'I'm so sorry,' said Fergus nearly in tears now himself.

'No, Fergus,' said James, 'thank you for bringing these to me. He took a deep breath and wiped his face with his sleeve.

The two men sat looking at the picture of Tegan and Nigel kissing.

'Who took it?' asked James.

'Did her camera have a timer switch?'

'Yes, yes it did.'

'It looks like it was just two of them there.'

James looked away for a moment and at the boxes of her clothes. He had finally taken them out of her side of the wardrobe last month, but as he had folded the delicate dresses into the boxes, he could almost feel her petite waist between his hands and had lost the heart to give them away. He'd kept them there in the sitting room. Could it be true? Tegan and . . . Nigel? If she had run off to be with him, why was he still here?

'Do you know him?' asked Fergus.

James nodded, then got up suddenly and went to the telephone in the hallway, leaving Fergus in the sitting room. He picked up the little phone book and flipped to B, found Nigel's number written in Tegan's handwriting. He held the receiver and dialled.

'Nigel? James Deane here.'

'Ah James, good to hear from you, old pal. How are you these days?'

'Were you and Tegan . . .' James's voice broke and he stood for a moment with the receiver to his ear. 'I have these photos of you and her up at the lake . . .'

'What are you talking about, James? Have you been at the cooking sherry?'

'Nigel, I have a photo of you two kissing.'

The line went dead.

James replaced the receiver in its cradle, returned to the sitting room and looked at Fergus. 'He hung up.'

'Do you think he might know something about her disappearance?'

'I don't know. I feel sick.' All these years he wanted answers and now he didn't want to think about it. How could she betray him like that?

'I think you should ring the police,' said Fergus.

James stayed standing with his hands on the table and stared at him. 'And say what exactly? You think the police are going to believe your story about the lens . . . I'm not sure I even believe it.'

Fergus looked around at the boxes. 'No,' he said decisively. 'You're going to tell them you found the photographs in the attic, hidden with her things.'

James was still for a moment. Then he exhaled and nodded. The attic story seemed plausible and it wasn't too far from the truth. He sat down.

'I think you should go to the police right away. Especially as you've told Nigel you have photos. Have you got an envelope?'

James looked around the desk for one, then paused and dug through one of the boxes of clothes. He pulled out an old Woolworth's bag and held it up.

'Even better,' said Fergus. He scraped up a full set of the photos and put them into the bag. The copies he put back in the box and into his backpack. He took the lens out and left it on the table next to the Woolworth's bag. 'I'm going to leave now so that you can go and do that. Will you be okay, James?'

'Yes. Thank you.'

'Are you sure?'

James inhaled deeply and nodded. 'Yes.' Then he turned around suddenly and grabbed an album from the bottom of a pile. He followed Fergus out to the front door.

'This is for you,' he said, pushing the album into Fergus's hands. 'Go to the Strand in London. To this stamp dealer . . .' He grabbed a pen and notepad from the telephone table and wrote down a name. He opened the album to the first page and pointed at the first stamp, the reverse steam train. 'This one will take care of your expenses of getting here, and plenty more besides for quite some time.'

'I can't take this.'

'I'll never sell them. What good are they sitting in an album? It's time I let go of them.'

'But—'

'They were never mine to begin with.'

'What do you mean?'

'Never mind. Just take them.'

'Thank you.' Fergus put the album into his backpack.

'Thank you, Fergus.'

From the sitting-room window James watched Fergus walk away. Then he pulled on his wool blazer and picked up his keys.

Nigel wasn't in when the police called at his house. They searched it and found a lock of Tegan's hair. They found other locks of hair, too. They headed for the lake with dogs and shovels and cordoned off an area populated with shrubs just in from the grassy shoreline.

Negatives are difficult to distinguish unless we hold them up to the light. When we pass light through them on to photographic paper, they form a latent image which it is our job to then make visible.

London

Britain's capital is full of famous streets, historic buildings and landmarks. Let us take a tour of some of them.

| We are stone |
We are stone	We are silent
We are stone	We are silent	We are hard
We are stone	We are silent	We are hard	We hear you
We are stone	We are silent	We are hard	We hear you	We see you
We are hard	We feel you	We are silent	We hear you	We see you
We feel you	We are silent	We are hard	We see you	We know you
We hear you	We see you	We know you	We feel you	We are hard
We know you	We are hard	We hear you	We see you	We are silent
We are silent	We are hard	We hear you	We see you	We know you
We see you	We feel you	We know you	We are silent	We hear you
We are hard	We are silent	We feel you	We hear you	We know you

We are what the paths beneath your feet are made of, the walls you lean against, the monuments you build to men. The pedestals you put them on. We are cold in winter, cold enough to freeze the homeless, hot enough in summer to send your sight wobbling with waves of doubt in what you see. We are absorbent. We are unyielding. We are still. Some of us have come from faraway places, others were hewn from the land right here. Some of us are angular and carefully measured, some of us have been chipped away at to reveal shapes, some of us are smooth and shining, some are rough. We are many colours, pink and brown and black and white and so many shades, shades that come from the changing whims of the earth, melting us and cooling us and swallowing and regurgitating us, compressing us and wearing us down and breaking us apart, and moving us along with wind and water and throwing us against each other, constantly forming and reforming us until one day people took us, cut us into shapes and placed us in this metropolis, made us a part of it, trying to freeze time, trying to make the changing world static, as if it is possible to make something permanent. We are solid. Strong. Unique. Tough. Privy to everything.

Imagine you and all the people are one entity. A being that can be chiselled apart into smaller separate beings, without pain or complications or identity crises; that is what we are. We can be molten, solidified, compacted, broken down, pulverised, but we never cease to exist. You humans bloom and whither almost all at once.

London Airport (Flint)
A trip to London airport makes for an exciting day out. From the public enclosure we watch with awe the magnificent aeroplanes take off and land, while information about the flights is given

over the loudspeakers: the type of plane, its origin and destina-
tion. The names of distant places set our imaginations racing.
Sometimes the names of important passengers are announced.

She is leaving one part of the earth and going to walk on
another because she thinks she will not follow herself. She
believes the thoughts of him, the pain of leaving him will not
come with her. I feel it all through the soles of her feet; the soul
of her pours into us every time she treads the ground and it
rises with her when she lifts her foot from us again.

I am formed from the sediments of my siblings. Three thousand years ago I was carved into a point, chipped away at by
humans who used my siblings for tools. I was given a human
function. I was given the power to kill at their command.

An arrowhead, I flew through the air strapped to a stick. I
punctured the skins of boars, plunged into their warm bodies, entered lungs, intestines, kidneys; my body absorbed their
warmth as their hearts slowed and stopped. Wiped clean, I
was used over and over. Until a human shot me into vegeta-
tion and I lay untouched for a thousand years.

Romans in sandals marched over me.

Then came the people who stayed. They built cottages and
called my resting place and theirs Hetherewe. One of their
young dug me up, pocketed me. A jewel he called me and
carried me with him. Left me one day out on the heath and
never came back.

Not long ago now, Sixteen String Jack knelt on me while
hiding in Highway Man's Lair. Many times his turmoil and
fear and excitement dropped invisible roots into me as he
readied himself, whispering in solitary rehearsal 'Stand and
deliver'.

200

Horses trod me into the ground, then the ploughs they pulled churned me back up. The roots of fruit trees bypassed me.

Then came the people who think they can leave us. They disconnect from the earth like magic in winged metal tubes. They uncovered some of us that had not been near the air in hundreds or thousands of years. Turned us into parts of buildings, into roads. Me they made part of gravel. And she is the last one to step on me. Through brand-new sandals that chafe her feet.

Some time after she steps on me, someone gasps. They lift me. Brush me. Examine me. Hold me on the soft pads of their fingertips. Admire me. Marvel at my endurance. Place me in Perspex. I am disconnected from my kin. No matter. This building, too, will fall, and I will return to my brethren in no time at all.

Kew Gardens (Brick)

Kew Gardens is one of the most famous gardens in the world. Besides the millions of different kinds of plants and flowers there are many interesting buildings to see, such as enormous glasshouses, a palace called the Dutch House and the Chinese Pagoda.

I was made as a folly. Rain bites at me, and held together by cement I need upkeep and repair a few times a century just to stop me falling apart, but people still marvel at me. I'm not Chinese, not by a long shot. I'm supposed to be seven storeys high – one for each step to heaven. I am ten. But I did once help someone get to the beyond. I seemed a sacred, familiar thing to him.

Once I was surrounded by other follies: the Moorish Alhambra, the Turkish Mosque, the Palladian Bridge and the Menagerie. We were fashionable. The others were all taken down, but me they kept – perhaps because of the views afforded by my height. I am a tool with which to see the treetops and the foliage. They left a great long grassy walkway leading to me so that people can admire me as they approach.

The man who found his way to the beyond through me saw me for something important and noble. Though he was not really a man; he was a man-spirit. He came here attached to a young woman, a down-and-out, as the Garden Constabulary call them. She walked up the avenue towards me, barely seeing me, seeming to be more absorbed by the grass between her toes but he, he floated above her attached by gossamer threads, and he regarded me with awe. He strained towards me, but as the woman turned and walked another way he went with her. A man approached the down-and-out woman. A living man. A man who works here, measuring wind and rain. They looked at the sky and pointed, and just before a thunderstorm spilled rain and light and sound, they went into the building that is glass, glass, glass – sand melted and turned solid and transparent. The man and woman and the man-spirit came back out and so did the sun and when they did they stood and talked. She turned slowly with her eyes closed and as she did the man-spirit came undone.

He left the woman and floated to me and when he entered me it was a sort of homecoming. He rose, spiralling up my centre, storey after storey, and with each one he became lighter and lighter and when he came to the final roof he passed through it. He lodged a moment in the spire where he glowed twice with the brightness of 10,000 candles and then he was gone.

Westminster Abbey (Red Sandstone)

Westminster Abbey is home to the coronation chair. It is on this throne that our kings and queens sit to be crowned. Underneath the seat is the ancient Stone of Scone, which used to be used for the coronation of the kings of Scotland. It is also known as the Stone of Destiny.

I'm used to carrying weight, the weight of years, the weight of land, of rivers, of silt and clay and pebbles. I have been all those things and all those things have made me. I was cut and carved to cradle the rumps of royalty. Men pierced me with metal and attached two rings to carry me. I held the haunches of kings up north. Where it is colder. For many years that is where I was until someone came and took me south, put me in this ornate cavernous building and kept me here. Decided I was his, as if any man can own anything.

Not many years later some young people took me, a fugitive, back to the north. They dropped me in the process, cracked me in two and I became a royal we. Patched me together, poured whisky over me. Though there is so much more of me they could cut out of the land, it is this me, this block, that is important to them.

I was returned to this place. I am housed under an elaborate wooden seat. Boxed in, but visible. They no longer sit directly on my surface. Standing before me, a tall man with ridges in his brow like those in the muds that formed me. He is from where I am from.

He did not come to this city just to see me. He is looking at me and thinking of destiny. Leaking from him, into the floor and into me, are the grief and relief he brought with him from the last place he stood and looked. It takes time for the feelings to dissipate. The colonnades, vaulted ceiling and chequered floors have come with him. Floating around him are 24,000 men's names, some of them his friends; he is thinking of all those men in the sea, their bones and teeth becoming sand.

He is thinking how fitting it is that the garden was sunk. His feet are feeling the solidity of solid ground. The battles did not get him, nor the walls an inscription of his name. He is wondering what destiny led him to be able to walk away from the memorial of graveless men, to be able to take in the sight of me, to be able to walk all over the pavements of this city, to tour the monuments and buildings and be as alive and anonymous as anyone. He is wondering what destiny lies ahead of him and his kin.

I will not be here much longer. These rings invite people to lift me and move me again.

Parthenon Gallery (Marble)

The British Museum in Bloomsbury is huge and full of artefacts from all over the world, some of which are over three thousand years old! For those who are interested in ancient civilisations, the Elgin Marbles are not to be missed. These are statues from the Parthenon, an ancient temple dedicated to the Goddess Athena, built in Athens in around 432 BC.

We are a stone hoard, a horde of amputees and mutilated pieces. We recline without hands or feet. Heads cracked off; armless, legless torsos; a single half foot; a bodiless head, its face chipped off. Then there are the half ones, the temple relief ones, nascent figures rising out of marble, like story-book illustrations emerging from walls. Processions of people and horses half-formed, lapiths locked in battle with centaurs, cattle being led to sacrifice.

I, a caryatid, once held with my five sisters a roof on our heads. Now there's nothing to carry. I was shaped by mallet and chisel. Filed and polished so that the Hellenic sun brought out a golden glow in my flawless white skin. It is my translucence that you value because it gives the impression of human skin. It is the impression of human skin that is unsettling. Even without forearms I am sublime.

He comes to ogle our parts. He brings his notebook, but he is not like the artists. He looks at us differently. He has something else in mind. He studies my form, his hands dancing in the air in front of him as if he is imagining forming me, creating me, hands slightly cupped move up and down, undulating in and out with my battered noseless stone face, neck, shoulders, breasts, waist, hips, down my legs and back up. He fills in the gaps. My body is an insinuation under my peplos, pinned at the shoulders. Funny how easily men are tricked by these illusions (there is only a gown, no body behind it, just more me, more marble).

He quotes Aristotle: 'The chief forms of beauty are order, symmetry and clear delineation.' Then he turns to her. Sets his hands dancing in the air before her shape. She is slight, like a boy. He is educating her, pointing to this and that and explaining things to her as if to a child though she is not a child. Her body is not strong like mine, but it is lithe. Her hair is long and loose and red. Mine is ornate in its intricate braid, but hers moves. She has hands. She has real legs beneath her skirt. She has the means to walk away from him – there is menace in his hands and in his eyes – but she will not. She is no Amazon. She does not know the power of women. She has not even heard of Athene.

'In portraying the ideal types of beauty,' he reads from his notebook, 'you bring together from many models the most beautiful features of each. That's Socrates,' he says. He puts an arm around her waist and leads her on.

Egyptian Sculpture Gallery (Granodiorite)

It is impossible to run out of intriguing things to see at the British Museum. There are some treasures we must be sure not to miss. We must look at the Rosetta Stone, which dates back to 196 BC. It was from the writing on this stone that scholars learned how to read ancient Egyptian writing.

An old man stands before me with a young girl, his granddaughter. The girl holds his hand and asks him what I am.

I am older than ancient, though that is all you think of me. You think that before those polyglots scratched my surfaces I was nothing. My cousins form other planets, the highlands of the moon, the crust of Mars and you think because a man could read three scripts he is powerful. Even crushed, my kind carry your cars. I have been so close to the core of the earth that I have melted.

This sparkling crystalline structure of mine took patience – I stayed under the surface cooling slowly away from the air, waiting, allowing myself to become magnificent.

I would still be lying inside a mountain by a river had they not found me and cut me away from the whole, from the rest of me. They cut me to the size of a man, polished my front to a plane and left my back rough. Priests gathered around me with words of praise for a man they worshipped. They chipped away bits of me to list his good deeds in languages everyone could understand. He is dead thousands of years. I live on.

I stood in their building of worship until it fell and I was taken to another place after which they named me. There I stood, solid and unshakeable, side by side with others to hold walls up in a building they called strong until men took me away, brought me across the sea, claiming me as theirs, thinking they could own me. They pressed wax and ink and water and paper to me, made copies of my scratches, stared at them until they made sense.

People look at me in awe because I bring three of their languages together, allowing them to understand and communicate. I am a key, a portal through which words from the past come to people in the present. I give them access to worlds they could not see into, could not connect with, could not read before.

'You are like the stone,' the old man tells the young girl. 'Before you came along your daddy and mummy and I could not talk to each other. Not properly. We didn't know how. We three were separate. You brought our worlds together.'

I remind the old man of another engraved stone he sometimes stands before. A stone that brought him peace and pain at the same time. A stone he has stood before with this girl, and this girl's parents. 'Your grandma would be very proud of you,' he tells the girl. 'Shall I tell you a secret? I think that when you and your mummy play the harp, your music floats all the way up to your grandma and she can hear it.' The girl smiles at her grandfather, tugs his hand and they move on.

Piccadilly (Yorkstone)
Piccadilly is one of the widest and straightest streets in London. It runs all the way from the bright lights of Piccadilly Circus at one end to the grassy peacefulness of Hyde Park at the other. It is worth going for a stroll here to marvel at its many fine old houses and hotels.

I am sixty million years old. I look well for it, though most people never look down to see me. In this form I am a mere three hundred or so years old. I was bright when they cut me, cut us, into flat squares and laid us beneath your feet. Weather and human drudgery, legions of hurried heavy footsteps soon darkened my surface.

I contain crystals but you never stop to see them. I know you contain treasures, too, all of you, but most of you don't stop to see those either.

There are many of us, and so, so many of you. We stretch on, linked to one another, laid flat and smooth side by side, carrying your feet all the way along the sides of your streets. We are durable, we take the weight of you, of your emotions, let them roll from one of us to the next and the next.

She walks on us with a suitcase, full of bravery, fear and confusion. Enters one of the shimmering hotels. Later comes out without the suitcase and dripping down into us is a terrible excitement. She thinks she is free but eleven silver strings she cannot see trail slack behind her. She walks and she walks and goes into a place buzzing with people. When she comes out later, music spills out of the door as she opens it, and the trembling notes slather over and into us and her steps are unsteady but the fear is gone from them. Singing along to the fading song she begins to dance and her pleasure pours into us like nectar and it is worth carrying the weight of many people just to feel one dance on us. Next day she walks and walks, under lights, statues, buildings, buses, between the agitation of people who do not look twice at her. The sense of purpose in her feet wavers, hesitation comes in undulations, the silver strings tauten. She returns to the hotel before dark and does not come out until the next day when she walks and walks and no longer knows why she is here and the silver strings begin to tug on her. One more day and she exits the hotel with her suitcase and leaves it in front of a woman collecting coins in a cup. Then she willingly, achingly allows the silver strings to pull her all the way out of the city and into the air, westwards.

St Paul's Cathedral (Portland Stone)

St Paul's Cathedral is a spectacular building on Ludgate Hill. Designed by Sir Christopher Wren, its most striking feature is the enormous dome. It is breathtaking to stand underneath it and look up into it. We can even climb steps all the way up into the dome to the Whispering Gallery, where words whispered into the walls can be heard all the way around at the opposite side.

Death made me. Deceased marine life and dinosaur footprints are in me. Detritus of living things and shells rolled around on the seabed, joining, growing, sinking, condensing, until it became me: one solid, dense, huge mass. What you see is a grey stone wall with black flecks.

A young man, here early with his sticks, tapping out a funereal beat. He arrives before the crowds because he's still awake from the night before. He carries a photo of his mother with him though now he is the same age as she is. He sings to me a song his mother sang. He stands and palms me with both hands. Right where his mother stood, a pitiful figure, pale but for the dark marks encircling her neck. Her words continue to go around in deathly silence, *It was Nigel, it was Nigel.* She was here with the bearded man when she was alive. He whispered to her *I've killed people* and her giggles went round and round.

No confessional box necessary here; they whisper secrets to me. Offload them into the soft air. Sometimes I want to be a wall that overhears what it wants, not one that is subjected to onslaughts of love declarations, noises and inanities. Rarely do they say anything worth hearing so I rebound their words, their voices. Send them back, bouncing in straight lines once, twice, until they reach whatever ears are at the opposite side of my circular self.

Every now and then someone says something too good to let go.

The grey-bearded man placed his life-taking hands against me, palms flat; there was murder in his hands, his blood had taken blood. It pulsed against me. *I'm sorry, Tegan*, he whispered and round the words went. I fused his hands into my surface, petrified them, encrusted, encased them, with all the other dead things. What's another fossil, another few bones? He tried to pull away, but it did not work. His bearded face terrified, he whimpered. He tried to push away from me, but only sank his arms further in, now fully swallowed to the elbows. Calcium, silica, carbon. Humans wear their shells on the inside. He wept, but he did not scream for help. He whispered, *I'm sorry, I'm sorry*. The words circled round and round. *I'm so sorry.* He grew weak and tired, sagged and hung from his elbows, his lower half pressed against me, and as it did I melded with it, too. His repentant words got closer and closer to my own face until his lips touched my smooth surface and were silenced, turning to stone. His beard, too. His chin. His forehead. His whole face became fossil. His feet, too. I absorbed him completely so that all that remains on the front, on the outside, is a slight discolouration, a barely perceptible bump where his head had been. Run your fingers over it – you might feel it. His last words still circle the walls, inaudible to human ears now they have faded so much but still they go around: *I'm sorry Tegan. I'm sorry I killed. Please, please.* His words were enough. There was more death in his palms he was sorry for.

Acknowledgements

This book began its existence while I was studying at University College Cork and I am grateful to many people I met there. Thank you to: Eibhear Walshe and Mary Morrissy for all the feedback, guidance and support; Jools Gilson for encouraging me to experiment; Brendan Mathews and Zsuzsi Gartner for broadening my view of what fiction can be; Claire Connolly for her support; Ladette Randolph for her advice; Kathy D'Arcy for all the early morning *Shut Up and Write* sessions; my classmates and colleagues for everything I learned from them.

For financial support I am grateful to: UCC School of English for a scholarship that made my studies possible; the Irish Research Council for the life-changing opportunity awarded to me in the form of a postgraduate scholarship; Cork County Council Arts Office for a bursary which enabled me to redraft this book at the Tyrone Guthrie Centre – and thank you to all at the TGC for taking such good care of its residents.

In getting this book from my desk out into the world I am grateful to: Ludo Cinelli for his energy, enthusiasm and efficiency, and to Eve White for bolstering this; Becky Walsh for her expertise and guidance, and also to Martin Bryant for his eye for detail.

I am grateful to those friends I called on to double-check my jazz fusion, photography, seaweed, beverages, wording of bits of dialogues, and providing the kind of help and advice that only they can. To my family and friends for the various ways in which they lend me support and encouragement – heartfelt thanks.

Author's Note

The fabricated quotations, in italics, throughout this book were inspired by Ladybird Books, which were a formative part of my, and indeed many people's, early reading experience. The amount of expert information conveyed in the distinctive Ladybird tone continues to surprise and delight me as an adult reader. I could never hope to match the wonderfully unique and inimitable wording of those vintage books. Hence the invented quotations that form part of the narrative of *Catchlights* are written not so much to emulate, but rather to pay homage to the phenomenon that was and is Ladybird Books and the world that they created for many generations of young readers.

ORIGINALS

NEW WRITING FROM
BRITAIN'S OLDEST PUBLISHER

2021

Penny Baps | Kevin Doherty
A beautifully-told debut about the relationship between brothers and the difference between good and bad.

'Doherty brings a new, indeed original voice to the Irish fiction table, a voice that he has clearly nurtured like Cahir's trees' *Irish Times*

A Length of Road | Robert Hamberger
A memoir about love and loss, fatherhood and masculinity, and John Clare, by a Polari Prize-shortlisted poet.

'An emotionally intelligent writer whose work is rooted in people and relationships' Jackie Wills

We Could Not See the Stars | Elizabeth Wong
To discover the truth about his mother, Han must leave his village and venture to a group of islands which hold the answer to a long-held secret.

'There is really no book quite like it' A Naga of the Nusantara

2020
Toto Among the Murderers | Sally J Morgan
An atmospheric debut novel set in 1970s Leeds and Sheffield
when attacks on women punctuated the news.

'An exhilarating novel' Susan Barker

Self-Portrait in Black and White | Thomas Chatterton Williams
An interrogation of race and identity from one of America's
most brilliant cultural critics.

'An extraordinarily thought-provoking memoir' *Sunday Times*

2019
Asghar and Zahra | Sameer Rahim
A tragicomic account of a doomed marriage.

'Funny and wise, and beautifully written' Colm Tóibín, *New Statesman*

Nobber | Oisín Fagan
A wildly inventive and audacious fourteenth-century Irish
Plague novel.

'Vigorously, writhingly itself' *Observer*, Books of the Year

2018
A Kind of Freedom | Margaret Wilkerson Sexton
A fascinating exploration of the long-lasting and enduring
divisive legacy of slavery.

216

'A writer of uncommon nerve and talent' *New York Times*

Jott | Sam Thompson
A story about friendship, madness and modernism.

'A complex, nuanced literary novel of extraordinary perception' *Herald*

Game Theory | Thomas Jones
A comedy about friendship, sex and parenting, and about the games people play.

'Well observed and ruthlessly truthful' *Daily Mail*

2017
Elmet | Fiona Mozley
An atmospheric Gothic fable about a family living on land that isn't theirs.

'A quiet explosion of a book, exquisite and unforgettable' *The Economist*

2016
Blind Water Pass | Anna Metcalfe
A debut collection of stories about communication and miscommunication – between characters and across cultures.

'Demonstrates a grasp of storytelling beyond the expectations of any debut author' *Observer*

The Bed Moved | Rebecca Schiff

Frank and irreverent, these stories offer a singular view of growing up (or not) and finding love (or not) in today's uncertain landscape.

'A fresh voice well worth listening to' *Atlantic*

Marlow's Landing | Toby Vieira
A thrilling novel of diamonds, deceit and a trip up-river.

'Economical, accomplished and assured' *The Times*

2015
An Account of the Decline of the Great Auk, According to One Who Saw It | Jessie Greengrass
The twelve stories in this startling collection range over centuries and across the world.

'Spectacularly accomplished' *The Economist*

Generation | Paula McGrath
An ambitious novel spanning generations and continents on an epic scale.

'A hugely impressive and compelling narrative' John Boyne, *Irish Times*